CAPTIVE TO HER FATED MATE

EXOTIC PACK SHIFTERS 3

LEELA ASH

PAMELA AVERY

CONTENTS

CHAPTER 1

Sheryl Quinn knew this trip was straight from hell.

First, her back tire had picked up a nail just outside civilization with no help in sight and she had had to change it herself — a chore she vastly hated. Next, her car overheated a few miles back, and she had to wait for it to cool off before topping the radiator with water; she'd been pulling over nonstop for the past few miles, thanks to that. Then, apparently, because her day hadn't gone badly enough, the last time she'd needed to refill her water, she had also tried to answer the call of nature in some nearby bushes only to miss her footing, topple down the low sloping hill, and end up in a crumpled heap of sand and grasses. Her pants had gotten ripped at the knees, her white shirt was a sorry brown mess and her once beautiful curly hair now rivaled a bird's nest. She had ripped off the shirt, leaving her tank top on, and finger-combed her hair into some semblance of order. Her pants were still torn, though, leaving her looking like some teenage groupie wannabe, she thought with a grimace as her eyes strayed to her dashboard to check the temp for the umpteenth time.

Now her gas was edging dangerously low, she noticed, with a feminine grunt of displeasure as she passed the signpost for a charming little town called Angel Springs.

"Angel my ass," she grumbled. "I bet these townsfolk are about as angelic and welcoming as briar bushes."

"Don't cuss. I can hear you all the way from Arizona," a breathy female voice laughed, the tone teasing.

The disembodied voice came from the phone on the seat beside Sheryl. That was her sister, Kate, whom was still on the line with the phone on speaker. Sheryl had set her iPhone on the passenger seat beside her, allowing her to talk to her sister while she drove.

Sheryl sighed, "My bad. I'm not on speaker, am I?"

She heard Kate chuckle, "Marissa is too busy with her dolls to notice if she's the one you're worried about. And if it's me you're worried about, then, by all means, cuss away. Just jerking your chain. My 'tender sensibilities' can take the strain," Kate joked.

Sheryl turned off the highway and drove her battered Mazda toward the gas station with the words *Angel Gas* printed boldly over the station.

Her lips quivered a little at the unlikely name, and she smothered a laugh. Her sister picked up on the slight lift in her mood and queried immediately, "What? See something funny on your road trip?"

"How about, 'Angel Gas'?" Sheryl tossed out.

"No!" Kate snorted over the line as Sheryl dissolved into outright laughter.

The beaming gas attendant, a slim boy with ears that were too big, extra-long limbs he had yet to grow into, and a friendly face, came up to her. "Welcome to Angel Gas, ma'am."

Sheryl nodded as she turned off the ignition and threw him a grin, "Angel Gas, huh?"

He looked confused for a minute, then he shrugged, "Well, yeah. That's what it says on the signboard."

She sighed, stifling the urge to roll her eyes. He still didn't get it. No sense debating whether angels had gas or not, she supposed.

She gave him her cash and watched as he filled her tank. As soon as he was done, she drove her car to a corner of the gas station and climbed out to walk the short distance to peer through the display glass of the store windows in the gas station. Rows of bright-colored chocolates and cookies stared back at her.

"Sheryl?" Kate's voice came over the phone clutched in her hand.

"Right. Sorry. Window shopping. Literally," Sheryl replied, returning the phone to her ear as she turned off the speakerphone.

"Yay, I definitely want some souvenirs," Kate crowed.

The reminder that this was supposed to be a fun vacation made her throat close up in despair, and for a minute, Sheryl was speechless.

Kate caught on almost at once, and she asked in a quiet tone, "You're not still thinking of that bastard, are you?"

"Hard not to," Sheryl replied honestly. "Especially since, right up until five days ago, *Le Bastard* was my fiancé, and we were supposed to take this road trip together and wind up in Las Vegas right in time for our Vegas Wedding. But no, that didn't happen because he got caught with his pants down right in the middle of the office I decorated just for him! I was such a romantic idiot!"

"You're still pissed," Kate observed.

"You think?" Sheryl sighed, feeling a band of tension contract in her chest. All right, time to ease up she told herself mentally. If she kept nursing these wounds, she could do some serious damage to herself, she thought absently stroking a hand down the middle of her chest.

"Sheryl, are you sure you should have gone on this trip all by yourself? If Sloan wasn't gonna come along, I don't understand why you didn't just cancel the trip," Kate sighed over the phone. "I mean, New York to Florida, and on to Vegas? That's a lot of miles. It's practically cross country, honey."

Sheryl grunted, "It was either that or sit around twiddling my thumbs and acting like the helpless woman. I can go on a fun trip just fine without *Le Bastard*. Besides, I didn't want to see him any time soon. I mean, it's practically a given that as soon as he was done banging his ... *other woman*, he was bound to come pleading. They always do that in the movies, right? I don't want to see his lying, cheating face anytime soon. I don't think I can handle seeing him again until I'm too old and feeble to do more than spit harmlessly in his direction."

Silence reigned for a bit through the phone, then Kate whispered, "You need to simmer down some, and maybe, um, try to talk through this. Maybe get a professional to listen, so you can really share how you feel?"

"What does it matter how I feel? I don't want to talk about it anymore," Sheryl yelled, suddenly so irate that she quite forgot she was standing outside. She was oblivious to the fact that she was also drawing the attention of the gas attendant and a new customer who had pulled up for a refill. "*Le Bastard* was nothing but a lying, cheating scumbag, and I think they deserve each other. I'm a twenty-first century woman, and I honestly don't need his company to enjoy my solo trip."

She felt tears well in her eyes, belying her words, and she blinked even as she silently acknowledged that the wound was still too fresh. Every time she shut her eyes, all she could see was her ex-fiancé, Sloan, grunting like a pig as he shoved his teeny-weeny dick, again and again, into Sally Howard's dirty little cunt. *They did deserve each other*, she thought with bleak humor, *the sleazy school principal and the slutty third grade teacher. So, what does that make me? The naïve kindergarten teacher who had been the last to know, that's what.*

The traitorous tears welled anew, and she blinked furiously to force them back down. No! She wasn't crying, she told herself furiously. Her eyes were just watering a lot; maybe because she wasn't used to the Florida heat or something?

As she looked around, trying to force down the tears she denied existed, her gaze clashed with a pair of strange-colored gold eyes burning with such heated intensity they seemed as though they had molten lava inside of them. The eyes with banked fire in them belonged to a very tall, striking young man who looked as though he had been observing her for a few minutes. But she hadn't seen him when she had pulled up, she thought with a frown, she would have remembered the sheer magnetism rolling off him in waves. She felt drawn to him mysteriously; everything about him seemed to compel her attention and seemed to want to draw her to him in some way she couldn't fathom.

His gaze was so compelling that she couldn't look away even to save herself and even as he stared into her eyes, a strange, almost hypnotic calm spread through her, ebbing away her anger but strangely leaving a rapidly growing tendril of lust in its wake.

His hair was a tousled mass of salt-and-pepper curls atop his head, and he was so strikingly handsome that it didn't seem fair to the poor female populace who had to behold such perfection. His shoulders were so wide and capable, his skin a deep golden tan as though he loved the outdoors, and his features were curved and regal. Something about him seemed almost animalistic, exotic and wild; something about him made her feel like Jane must have felt around Tarzan. The undeniable pull of attraction felt like a punch in the pit of her stomach; unwelcome but persistent.

A small pigeon chose that moment to land right at her feet and it waddled right up to her, pecking at the ground beside her. It pecked at her small toe too, unafraid and heedless of danger, before lifting itself a little into the air and flying straight to perch on the roof of the stranger's car. It hopped from his car roof onto his shoulder, then flapped its wings and took off.

It was the strangest thing, but even with the pigeon's antics, they hadn't been able to look away from each other for a minute, and yet, she sensed he was as aware of the pigeon as she had been. If she believed in superstitious nonsense, she would have wondered if there was some hidden meaning in there somewhere; as though the pigeon had drawn some invisible line connecting them.

Something indefinable shimmered in the air around them as they stared at each other, and Sheryl had to mentally remind herself to breathe, forcing her mouth open a little to take in much needed oxygen since her nostrils seemed to have closed up.

His gaze dropped to her slightly parted lips, raw fire kindling in their depths until she was almost afraid he would singe her with his gaze.

Sappy much? her subconscious sneered. *And so soon after that Sloan bastard too?*

Her spine straightened in remembered ire at the entire male population, and she very deliberately jerked her gaze away from the stranger's. She rudely turned her back on him and returned her gaze to the display beyond the shop windows. But even with her back turned, she could feel his every move with the intensity of a physical caress. She felt the exact moment he stopped boring holes into the back of her head with his eyes. She felt the exact moment he turned away to focus that laser gaze on the hapless gas attendant.

She started to sneak another look at him over her shoulder when the motion knocked the phone out of her hand, and it headed straight for the hard concrete beneath her feet. Before it could hit the ground, though, the man who had been standing a few feet away and hadn't even been looking at her, was beside her in a flash. He smoothly grabbed the phone, catching it just inches from the ground.

Sheryl knew her mouth had to be open like a fish's, but she couldn't help it. She had never seen anyone move that fast. One minute, he had been several feet away and the next, he was right beside her, catching her phone in his big fist.

Her widened eyes jerked upward to his and she started at the chagrin in his gaze even as his masculine scent assailed her nostrils. He seemed almost as though he were cursing himself inwardly for coming to help her.

Up close, his eyes were even more intense and lust-inducing than she had previously thought. Sheryl swallowed and took a quick step back for self-preservation.

He handed her the phone silently, and without a word, turned around and walked back to his car as he called out something to the gas attendant. The man's husky baritone caused her skin to sizzle in reaction, birthing goosebumps, as he thanked the gas attendant politely. Then, in mere seconds, he was gone, leaving her to risk one glance over her shoulder at his departing sedan. What was it about that man that had shocked her to the very depths of her soul? What was it about him that had made her want to draw ever closer to him as though pulled on some invisible string by a magnet? She had felt almost as though she recognized him at some basic, primal level. She had felt such a sucker-punch of attraction that she would never have imagined possible, and it had taken every ounce of discipline imaginable to tamp down on her feminine instincts to give him the come on. She detested men right now, thanks to Sloan, didn't she? An unwanted attraction to some barrel-chested stranger in the middle of a road trip she should have been taking with her cheating ex-fiancé was *not* what the doctor ordered.

Wide-eyed, she stared after the cloud of dust in his wake, her heart still thudding loudly in her chest. She looked at the gas attendant. She was still a bit shaky in reaction as she rasped, "Who was that?"

He smiled at her, and he was still clueless as ever as he remarked, "Him? Mikey's a local. No one special. He's just one of those brothers manning Exotic Rescue."

There was nothing 'just' or even slightly ordinary about him, she thought, trying in vain to still the wild pounding of her heart and the erratic pulse of her veins.

She flicked the boy a confused look, "Exotic what, now?"

"It's an animal shelter here in Angel Springs. They house exotic animals, like lions, bears, wolves, you name it. One time, when I was a kid, I coulda sworn I saw a dragon there. It's a very interesting setup they have there. You should check it out before you leave town. Gosh, it's so popular that I thought the whole world musta heard of it by now," he finished guilelessly.

Sheryl shook her head dismissively, even though her interest had been piqued, "Sorry, kiddo. Never heard of it. It ain't Disney Land."

Then, with one last glance at the now-empty road Mikey had disappeared down, she returned to her own car and slammed the door.

"Mikey sounds yummy," Kate opined as soon as she heard the door slam, indicating that her sister was once more alone.

"If by yummy you mean rude Neanderthal type guy who doesn't know when to stop staring, then, yeah, that's him,"

Sheryl said dismissively, deliberately throwing her sister off the scent.

Kate's sigh of disappointment was proof it had worked, which was just as well. Kate was a matchmaker without apology. Why, the first time she had visited Sheryl in her old workplace in New York, she had taken a mental census of all the single men in the place and decided Sloan, the school principal, was the 'worthiest prospect' for her baby sister. She had actively begun matchmaking, and before Sheryl had known what was happening, Sloan was turning on the charm, and she was falling for him.

Well, not this time, she thought with such vengeance that she felt a start. Was she secretly angry at Kate? That would be unfair. All her sister had done was try to make sure she was happy and had a family of her own too. Kate had done nothing wrong, she thought remorsefully.

"Hey, kiddo. You're awfully quiet over there," Kate said.

Sheryl blinked back tears. Her sister was eerily perceptive, but she had been taken in by Sloan too. They all had.

With a shake of her head, she told her sister something she knew she would want to hear, "I think I might as well drive over to your place instead of going all the way to Las Vegas y'know? It's been months and months since we have seen each other anyway. I miss you guys."

Kate's scream of joy could have woken the dead, and it took several minutes of reassurance for her sister to believe she wasn't shitting her about rerouting her trip to Arizona.

"But isn't that quite a drive? I mean, who wants to spend over thirty hours on the road alone with their thoughts?" Kate asked.

"Me, that's who. I need the downtime, Kate" Sheryl confessed.

Kate understood immediately as Sheryl had known she would.

As she finally hung up the phone with a sad smile, Sheryl reasoned that something good at least had come out of the entire trip: she could go see Kate and Marissa. Maybe once she saw her family, she could forget that her love interest of over three years had screwed her over and hadn't felt an ounce of guilt as he did so. She could forget that, once more, she had failed at something she badly wanted to win at. She could forget —

Darn it, why did her eyes keep watering? Damn Florida heat!

"Everything okay, ma'am?" the chirpy gas attendant asked, poking his cheery face in her side window again.

Sheryl forced a smile, "Just peachy."

He nodded, "Well, you might want to get a move on since it's coming on to dusk in about two hours. Or you could pick up some lodging in town and drop off your car here so we can fix that radiator for you. You *would* have a much smoother ride tomorrow when you leave if you didn't have to stop and refill after every hill."

Of course! It hadn't even occurred to her to see a mechanic about her radiator, which went to show how upset and distracted she truly was. She looked around, "Is there a workshop around here?"

He jerked his head toward a mechanic workshop just next door, and she smiled in gratitude. This town wasn't so bad after all. Angel Gas or no, the young man had been very helpful.

"What's your name?" she asked as she fished out a twenty-dollar bill; he deserved a tip.

"Tim, ma'am. Tim Jackson. My dad's the local sheriff," he added, grinning from ear to ear as he took the tip. "Thanks for the tip, ma'am."

"And I suppose 'round these parts, that gives you the seal of authenticity, huh? That must help with the girls," she added with a teasing grin as the boy ducked his head, while the tips of his ears went bright red. "Know a safe hotel I can stay in tonight?"

He nodded eagerly, "Just drive straight down and take the first turn on your left. Susie Bones is gonna be right there on your left and best part is, it's not that far from Exotic Rescue."

"Boy, you really love that animal sanctuary," she said with a shake of her head.

He shrugged, "What's not to love? There are some exotic creatures there, for sure."

She wrinkled her nose at him, "Fine, I'll bite. It's still bright enough that I can see my own nose. I'll explore a little once I've checked into Susie's. How would my car be delivered to the mechanic back here, though?"

He grinned and shrugged, "Easy. I get off in two minutes so I can totally drive it back here," he added, eyeing the car in that way young adults do when they are just dying to get behind the wheel of a car.

Sheryl bit back a grin as she nodded and watched him clamber into the front passenger seat, all long limbs and awkward movements. As she let him guide her toward Susie Bones', Sheryl reflected that it seemed like a good enough small town. But years of reading romances had taught her that so many small towns had their deep dark secrets. She was willing to bet Angel Springs had tons.

Luckily, she wasn't planning on hanging around long enough to find out what the town's secrets were. She already knew it had hunks with molten lava for eyes and a penchant for eavesdropping; she didn't want to get drawn into any more drama, thank you very much.

Once this kid got her radiator fixed, she was blowing out of town faster than the earliest cock could crow. There was nothing for her here.

A niggling of doubt trailed through her mind at that last thought as a pair of molten colored eyes played on the edge of her vision. Sheryl frowned. What was it about Angel Springs that tugged at her heart and made her feel as though there was more to the little town than met the eyes?

CHAPTER 2

$\mathcal{M}$ichael Bennet stood still as a statue in the shrubs, tense and alert, as he waited for a clear view of the man he was supposed to be spying on. Roy Davison was his arch enemy, and while Michael was normally laidback and accepting of most people, he managed to dredge up enough energy to detest Roy with as much passion as Roy probably detested him.

Roy had to be the oldest and worst enemy of the entire Exotic Pack, and since Michael had had the unenviable task of being the one to finish off Atlas Corning, Roy's maniacal vampire father, it stood to reason that Roy loathed him. Although, last he heard, Roy hated every member of the Pack, from Theodore to Connor to Darryl to Jonathan to Justin. He hated them all, but he had somehow found out that Theodore and Michael had killed Atlas, so he hated the two of them especially.

Michael's gaze was drawn to the manly shadow in the upstairs window of one of Susie Bones' rooms. He had set up surveillance over the past few weeks and had stumbled upon a secret stash of plans and diagrams that indicated that Roy was planning yet another attack on Exotic Rescue.

Exotic Rescue was the only home he and his five shifter brothers had known for as long as he could remember. Damned if he was going to stand by and let some vampire with a vendetta get the better of his home.

Michael knew he didn't have the luxury of time. He needed to uncover some of Roy's deep dark secrets *fast*. It was probably the only way to save the shelter and everyone he cared about. Sure, vampires were generally dangerous but as far as he could tell, Roy was even more dangerous because he had a chip on his shoulders about Michael and the rest of the Pack, and unlike other nocturnal vampires, he seemed to have developed the ability to walk in daylight without being fried extra crispy by the sun, just like Roy's father, Atlas Corning had been able to.

If Michael could discover his secret, maybe it could give them an edge in defeating Roy for good.

A few weeks ago, Roy had kidnapped Julia, killed her ex-boyfriend and planted enough bombs in Exotic Rescue to make quite an explosion. The damage would have been massive if Julia, Connor's new bride, hadn't escaped in time to warn them all.

Sick shifters were counting on Exotic Rescue to remain up and running because it was the one place they could easily get healed with the miracle-mineral on the land, Tailan.

Michael shook his head now as he reflected that no one would have imagined that Connor of all people would fall in love with such a feisty, smart, go-getter alpha shifter like Julia, especially since Connor himself was so alpha, aloof and averse to anything remotely resembling romance.

For that matter, Julia had also had a commitment phobia that rivaled Connor's, but when those two had finally gotten together, the sparks they produced could have lit up the freakin' Fourth of July without fireworks.

Thinking of fireworks drew his thoughts relentlessly to the curly-haired brunette he had run into at the gas station. She'd had such a sad, sad look in her troubled brown eyes and that seductive pout that puckered up her pink lips. She was pure dynamite; seductive without trying, magnetic without wanting to be. She had obviously been from out of town; her clothes, her slight accent and even her demeanor had screamed stranger. Maybe she was passing through? *It would be interesting to see her again*, he thought, shifting slightly. He would want to see if the evening sunlight could pick out highlights in her hair that formed a halo when she turned just so; he would want to see if her legs really went on for miles as they had seemed to, at first glance; it would be interesting to see if her waist were really so tiny that he could span it with a single hand. And dang if he didn't want to perceive that sweet scent of jasmine that had drifted up to his nostrils when he saved her phone.

Driving into that gas station and seeing her had made him feel almost like some cat on steroids. His Wolf had immediately began hungrily seeking expression, until he could have sworn it was clawing away at his insides struggling to be free. He had wanted to stand over her in his Wolf form and lick her cheeks until she laughed, and the sadness left her eyes. Something about her had sparked something wild and passionate and absolutely unrestrained inside him as well as something incredibly protective. At the same time, his entire being had seemed to grind to attention in reverence when he clapped eyes on her. Frankly, it had been all he could do not to grab her and haul her flush against his hard masculine body. He had wanted her in a way he wouldn't have thought possible. In that singular moment, he had wanted to grab her and hoist her over his shoulder like some conquering Neanderthal, and then he had wanted to take her to his lair and brand her with his touch and mark her so permanently that no one else ever touched her again. She had stirred everything animal and masculine inside him, and he'd wanted her with a kind of intensity he had never felt, not even on his first sexual encounter.

His thoughts made him check, and he frowned. Why was he so attuned to some strange woman who had done nothing but glare at him and make him feel like an eavesdropper? Why was he feeling all possessive of someone whose name he didn't even know?

As though he had conjured her with his thoughts, the exact same woman came striding around the side of Susie Bones', her curls bouncing with each step she took as she walked. She was tall, at 5'8", with skin like smooth alabaster — or at least the way he imagined alabaster would be since he had never seen the damn thing. Her complexion was a dusky shade of almost olive, her long legs were encased in high-waist jeans so tight it seemed as though she had been poured into them. The jeans cinched her tiny waist tantalizingly and were topped off by a white and black polka-dotted crop top that showed off a slice of satin skin just above her mid-riff. He noticed, at once, that she had changed out of her travel clothes. She looked breezier, fresher and somewhat less tense as though she'd just come from a shower. Thinking of her taking a shower was enough to send a shaft of lust burning through him with shocking intensity.

She is delectable, he thought, watching her sweep an absent hand through her curls as she walked with those long traipsing steps, obviously heading to the pool area a few feet away. A bright pink scrunchy held most of her curls away from her face and as she ran her hand through her curls, it tilted dangerously as though it might fall out but held fast.

He had a hard-on just watching her, he realized, cursing

inwardly as he looked downward at where his arousal had tented his fly. He stroked a hand uselessly trying to force it back down, but it jutted out proudly all the more as though seeking the promise of that warm, tight sheath it knew the woman he watched could provide. Her breasts rose proudly against the material of her blouse, and he traced the outline hungrily with his eyes. He gingerly took his hand away from his fly; it *wasn't* helping.

He cursed low under his breath. This was the last thing he needed right now. He was no monk, but he was on stakeout duty, dang it. If Connor or Theodore got wind of the fact that he had botched his surveillance of Roy because he had a hard-on for some stranger, they would skin him alive and probably neuter him while they were at it.

A low whistle, suspiciously like a signal, sounded in the bushes on his left, and he hunkered down in the shrubs he was hiding behind, his eyes scanning for the source of the sound. Sure enough, he saw two vampires standing beneath the shade of a tree, their gaze trained on the window he had been staring at a few minutes ago. He saw the curtains shift, and then the shadow in the room disappeared as the lights were turned off.

With lightning speed, Roy materialized a few feet away, grinning at the two vampires as they stepped out with caution from behind a tree.

Roy nodded at the men, "Gary, Lloyd. Took you two long enough."

The man he called Lloyd sniggered, "Well, I'm assuming you needed to see us urgent like, but you woulda had a hard time communicating if we had been roasted to a fine crisp by the sun first."

Gary sighed, "He means we had to wait for the sun to go down."

Roy ignored both of them and turned to head toward the pool, leaving them to follow.

Michael straightened in alarm. The woman was by the pool. He sure hoped they weren't planning on attacking her.

With a stealth honed from years of tracking and surveillance, he crept out of his hiding place, still taking cover behind some shrubs as he went.

Michael watched the men flick the woman a brief disinterested glance before taking their seats around a table a little farther away from her.

Michael saw the woman frown a bit as she regarded the three men, and he realized she'd sensed, at once, that something was off about them. *Smart woman! I knew I liked her*, he thought with silent approval.

Roy and his companions lowered their voices as they continued to talk, and Michael swallowed a curse. He couldn't hear them from all the way over here, and besides, he didn't want them or the woman to see him. *I really should have had Lynette come along with me*, he thought, thinking of the female shifter that was also a member of the Ops Unit he ran with Connor. Lynette could hear for miles in every direction. She would have picked up Roy's discussion with those two easily. Whoever they were, what they had to discuss with him had to be important because he had noticed Roy's restless pacing behind the curtains upstairs until he had heard the whistle signaling the arrival of his companions.

Itching to get closer, Michael started to inch behind a different shrub when Roy suddenly lifted his head and sniffed. He saw his two companions look a question at Roy as the other man shoved to his feet and began to look around angrily.

"What?" Lloyd demanded in a tone that carried loudly.

"Wolf," Roy growled. "I smell a Wolf."

Their eyes were scanning the entire terrain in suspicion, and Michael knew it was only a matter of time before he was found out. The edge of the building of the hotel blocked off where he had hidden beneath a shrub, so he straightened deliberately and strode out into view with studied nonchalance, making a beeline for the woman who was lounging nearby, a magazine clutched in her hands.

Roy threw him a disgusted look and then sank back onto his seat with his companions, apparently thinking he had merely picked up his scent because Michael had wandered by. It was exactly what he wanted him to think.

Michael strode right up to the woman and smiled with easy familiarity as he said, "There you are. Did you have a hard time finding this place?"

Her eyes narrowed with suspicion and then she shook her head mutely, refusing to say a word.

Great, I've freaked her out. She must think I'm a stalker. But I hadn't had much of a choice. It had been either I remain hidden until they sniff me out behind some shrubs, or I come out and act as though I'm here for some other reason.

He turned to Roy, and walked up to their table, keeping his voice in a low murmur that wouldn't carry to the woman, "This place must be losing its touch if they let people like you in now."

Roy was the proverbial cowboy type with bushy gray eyebrows, bloated mid-section, face flushed a deep red shade. Of course, his customary cowboy hat was still shoved onto his head. Michael had only childhood memories of Atlas to compare with, but it seemed to him, Atlas Corning had had a penchant for cowboy hats too, just like his son, Roy. Was it, perhaps, a safe bet to think that despite whatever it was that gave them the ability to walk in the sun, the sun's rays still affected them a little more than it affected normal humans or shifters? He mentally noted that clue as a vital key to cracking the code of what made Roy tick.

Roy bared his teeth in a parody of a smile as he retorted with a toss of his head that indicated the woman lying a few feet away, "*You* must be losing your touch. Crash and burn with the lady, huh?"

Michael growled, "Mind your own business."

With that, he turned around and strode away. Now, any 'lingering' scent Roy perceived of a shifter nearby would be attributed to the fact that there *had* been a shifter there a few minutes ago. Now, he could watch them, and they would be less on guard.

With a carefully masked grin of pleasure, Michael turned the corner of Susie Bones' to approach the pool area from the other side of the hotel. Roy and his companions had left the pool and were walking toward the parking lot, and he could make out the low murmur of their voices as they went. He was a few feet ahead, which meant they would run right into him if they came by. Quickly, he climbed into the branches of a large tree standing off to the side, and not a moment too soon because they came right by the tree almost at once, still deep in conversation.

"We need it, and fast, Roy," Lloyd garbled.

"He's right. Hard to raise an army if they cannot walk in daylight," Gary agreed.

Michael felt his heart still in his chest. They were talking about walking in daylight, which meant whatever Roy used to enable him to walk in daylight wasn't related to his blood connection to Atlas. It had to be something the other vampires thought they could get too. It had to be some sort of shrub, or plant, or material, or something external.

Just then, Roy laughed and held up his hand, letting the ruby ring on the small finger of his left hand catch the reflection of the lights lining the pathway. "It's a purty little thing, ain't it? But the materials for making it are hard to come by and very expensive too. Well, leave it to me. Theodore's money's finally gonna be good for something. I'll get it and make a ring for every bloodsucker who would march with me against those accursed abominations living it up in that pretentious sanctuary of theirs."

Michael felt like kissing the floor in thanksgiving. They had watched and waited for weeks on end to learn what made Roy able to walk in daylight and now he had gotten the information so cheaply? Why hadn't they thought of it? That ruby ring had always graced Atlas Corning's little finger during his fearsome days. Why had it never occurred to them that it might be more than a family heirloom?

Just then, a flash of movement off to the right caught his gaze and it was all he could do to keep from swearing a blue streak when he saw what it was.

That dratted, stubborn woman was bent at the waist as she peered through some hedges at the three men walking past, obviously trying to spy on them. *Who is she? She had seemed human enough to me, so why had she felt the need to spy on Roy and his cohorts?*

Or was she maybe a fairy, or gypsy, or something? If she hadn't been human, he would have sensed it, he thought.

Well, whatever she is, she is going to be dead and stretched in less than two seconds if Roy catches her listening in on their conversation, Michael thought as he deftly began to climb down the tree, careful to be as noiseless as possible.

Roy and the other men with him were laughing noisily as they reached into the trunk of a car and whipped out bags of blood. Roy skillfully flung one bag at Gary and grabbed one for himself, ripping it open and putting it to his lips.

Great, they wanted to feed. If they did, their senses would be heightened immediately, and they would pick out her smell and make her their meal.

Increasing his footsteps, Michael walked closer to the woman at the same time Gary brought out a large diamond sword and brandished it with an evil laugh in a wide showy arc.

The woman chose that moment to let out a small gasp and the three men froze. At the same time, Michael covered her mouth with his hand to keep her from screaming. She struggled against his hand, her eyes wide with fright as she looked up at him.

He leaned close to her ear and whispered, "Don't make a sound. I'm here to help."

She couldn't reply because her mouth was firmly covered but he read the response in her eyes, *Like hell.*

She began to struggle in earnest again just as Roy and his men started to come closer to the shrubs they were hiding behind.

He heard Roy snap, "Grab a fuckin' flashlight, right now. There's something behind that shrub."

With an inward curse, Michael looked at her again, "Forgive me."

He focused his laser gaze on hers, letting his wolf abilities shine through his eyes, staring into her eyes intently until his shifter powers overcame her human abilities and she slid into a deep sleep. He had always been able to calm people down; if he dialed it up a notch, he could push them into a Cinderella sleep right away.

Moving as fast as his abilities would allow, he zapped off a few yards with her and tucked her still body into a cozy nook in the wall of Susie Bones', effectively hiding her.

He saw Roy and his men searching furiously behind the shrub. He saw one of the men bend to pick something up and his eyes hardened as he realized what it was— her scrunchy. It must have fallen off.

He watched as the men held it out to each other and

sniffed it, passing her scent around. He knew what that meant; they suspected she had heard their secret, and now, they had passed her scent around, which was technically a vampire kill order. Gary tucked it into his back pocket and nodded at Lloyd and Roy before stalking toward his car. Lloyd went after him with long loping strides, and Roy stalked back toward the hotel, obviously intent on sniffing out his prey inside.

Great, now she was in more trouble than anyone had a right to be, Michael thought, looking down at the still unconscious woman. Since Gary had held onto that scrunchy, it meant, very soon, every vampire working with Roy would be sniffing that scrunchy to pick up her scent. If he let her go, she wouldn't last more than a night. And there was no way in hell he could take her to Exotic Rescue; she would raise a ruckus, and he would never be able to explain to her why she needed to be with him, nor would he be able to protect the secret of the shifters in the place. She was the curious sort and within two days of being there, she would be peeking through shrubs and hedges again.

He stared down at her as she remained unconscious. She looked almost like a little girl; so fresh and innocent.

Something inside of him stirred anew, an odd tenderness, a protective inclination. No matter what she thought of him, he couldn't let her be by herself. She would be killed in a heartbeat, and somehow, the thought of a world where she no longer breathed or lived left him feeling very cold— very cold indeed.

He stroked one small strand of hair off her forehead in an almost lover-like gesture. *There is no alternative,* he thought. *I would have to take her somewhere safe and far from everyone else for her own safety.*

But wouldn't that be like kidnapping her, his conscience protested.

There's no other way, his shifter side decreed more forcefully. *No matter how she feels about it when she comes around, being kidnapped is far better than being dead.*

Effortlessly, he rose to his feet with the woman in his arms, her limbs dangling. He would keep her with him for as long as it took for Roy to realize she was not a threat to him and to lose interest in her.

But how would he get *himself* to lose interest in her? Michael wondered as he watched her chest rise and fall.

Damnit!

CHAPTER 3

*S*heryl awoke with a low groan, reaching a hand up to where her head ached furiously. *Why did it feel as though horses had been stampeding through her skull?*

Her hands shook as she managed to sit up a little, looking around in confusion at the quaint, almost fairytale-themed interior of what looked like a cabin. *Where am I?* she wondered, trying to get her brain to work through the hazy fog.

She frowned. Last she recalled, she had been lodging at Susie Bones'. A flicker of memory intruded. No, that wasn't exactly right. She had been...

Where had she been? she wondered, fear rising palpably in her throat as she tried to recollect.

She raised a hand once more to calm the wild pounding in her head and that was when she saw it— a long rope was attached to her right wrist. She followed the line of the rope and found it attached to a huge immovable dresser a few feet away. Her eyes widened in alarm and her heart began to thud in her chest. What the hell?

She flicked a frightened glance at her left hand and

discovered she was also tethered to the window with that hand. Both her feet were tied more tightly and securely to the bed.

She was in *danger!*

Right on the heels of that realization, her memory came flooding back with a vengeance, her head pounding in resistance as her brain presented an unwanted memory of a pair of molten lava eyes that had seemed to shimmer with a very strange light as they stared intently into hers, and a clean masculine scent. That was the last thing she remembered. She had stared into his eyes, trying to shake off the sudden creeping feeling of drowsiness that had swept through her and the next thing she knew, she was waking up in some strange place.

Had he drugged me? she asked herself, frowning as she tried to recall if he had done anything remotely violent like try to knock her out with some substance or something. All she could recall was that intense hypnotic stare she hadn't been able to break to save her life.

Did he hypnotize me into sleeping then? How did I get here? What did he do?

She looked at her hands once more. The ropes binding them were loose enough that she could lift her hand to her head, but they were tight, at the same time, so that she couldn't hope to loosen herself. She couldn't lift herself off the scrawny mattress beneath her because the ropes binding her legs to the bedpost were very short.

She tried to scream but all that came out was a muffled sound. Her eyes widened in horror when she realized her mouth had been taped shut.

Dear Lord: had he kidnapped her?

As though in answer to her question, the door opened and the man from the gas station came in, carrying a pile of split wood. He was stripped to the waist, the muscles on his back rippling as he came, sweat dripping off his back and arms, and his piercing gaze was trained on her.

"You're awake now," he murmured.

'Get me out of these ropes!' she tried to scream. All that came out was a muffled *"Gerrr mm hmhm ro."*

He flung the firewood onto the ground in front of the fireplace and turned to face her. "I assume, by your frantic movements that you have something to say?"

Her eyes glared daggers at him, and he grinned. In spite of herself, her breath caught in her throat. When he smiled like that, his whole face lit up and he became even more unfairly attractive. He was a dangerous hooligan; how could she even find him remotely attractive, she wondered hysterically.

"Here's the deal," he was saying, oblivious to her turmoil. "I'm gonna remove the tape from your mouth—"

How kind, she spat inwardly with heavy sarcasm.

His eyes trained on hers, he continued, "But *don't* scream. You absolutely *cannot* scream. If you do, no one's gonna hear you anyway and no one's gonna come running, but I'm going to be very pissed."

Yeah right! People are gonna hear me and come running, she thought. *The only reason he would be pissed would be because he knows I only have to scream and it's game over for him. He's just trying to fool me into staying quiet.*

He was watching her carefully with an unreadable expression on his face. He tilted his head to the side as though assessing her ability to be obedient. Sheryl dropped her lashes and assumed a meek demeanor; or at least, what she hoped seemed like a meek demeanor.

He stared at her for a minute, then he said, "I'm taking off the tape. *Don't* scream."

She shook her head mutely, unconsciously copying her little niece, Marissa's technique when she swore solemnly not to do something that everyone knew she absolutely intended to do.

The moment he took off the gag, she threw back her head and belted out a scream that could have shattered glass.

She half-expected him to backhand her or try to shush her but, to her horror, he merely stood back and folded his arms, letting her scream herself hoarse.

A nagging suspicion snuck into her mind at his calm attitude, and her scream began to lose volume after almost five minutes of having at it.

He quirked one eyebrow. "Are you done? Gotten it out of your system yet?"

She glared, "Let me go."

"Not on your life," he replied.

"Please. What have I done to you? You don't even know me," she whispered.

He grinned, "Sure, I do. Sheryl Quinn, 26, schoolteacher, sister, introvert, former girlfriend to *Le Bastard,* empowered twenty-first century woman, hater of all men."

She glared. He might as well have added *Mother of Dragons* to the list with the way he had reeled out the information like he was reading Daenarys Stormborn's resume, she thought with dark humor. How she could think of *Game of Thrones* at a time like this was beyond her.

Her glare darkened as she realized that he had unashamedly owned up to eavesdropping on her conversation at the gas station because where else had he heard the 'empowered twenty-first century woman' bit and the '*Le Bastard'* term?

"Well, *you* haven't done anything to endear the male species to me, so you can't blame me," she informed him. "Let me go this instant."

"Or what?" he taunted.

She struggled helplessly against the ropes. Then she tried, "Or I'll scream."

He laughed at that one. "You already tried that option, didn't you, and you saw how well that worked out. Wanna go again? Go ahead, give it your best shot." He strode over to the curtains and flung them aside, "Welcome to nature, baby."

Sheryl's heart sank. They were right in the middle of what seemed to be a very thick forest. She didn't have to be a seer to know there was no one around for miles. No one was going to hear her or save her, even if she screamed through a megaphone.

She shot him a look that was half-timid, half-pleading, and in that instant, she almost despised herself. She didn't want to resort to begging. She had never been the weak, cowering type, and even if, by some accident, she had some weakness inside of her, Sloan had weaned her of that. "What do you want with me?" she demanded, hating the slight quiver in her voice.

He shrugged, "I want you to stay put."

It's like banging one's head against a wall, Sheryl thought, feeling real fear inside of her. He's a man, and here I am, a woman, alone, all bound and trussed up like Thanksgiving turkey. I'm completely at his mercy, and he's yet to say what he wants with me.

Oh Lordy, he isn't some sex pervert who yanks women off the streets and hurt them, is he? But something about him seems... Well, clean and decent. Almost comforting, really.

Her mind was addled, she thought angrily as she glared up at him. He had kidnapped her and spirited her away to God knows where, and she thought he was *decent?*

She frowned as another thought intruded, how long had she been out? The last time she had been self-aware had been evening, but now, it was morning.

Her stomach grumbled aloud, and he straightened at once, "You must be hungry."

As he padded away, Sheryl asked the question uppermost on her mind, "What day is it?"

He quirked an eyebrow, "Tuesday?"

"How long have I been out?"

"Since last night," he told her, watching her carefully.

Her mind was working fast as she considered her options. She was supposed to have called her sister last night after her car had been towed, and she was supposed to pick her car up this morning from the little workshop near Tim's garage. Surely, her sister and Tim Jackson would notice she hadn't shown up or called, and they would get the cops on her case. Getting the cops wouldn't be any sort of hardship for Tim since his father was the sheriff, she assured herself.

Swallowing, she tried that last track, "I don't know what you could possibly hope to gain from kidnapping me, but you should know that people will be looking for me."

His mouth quivered a little as though he were fighting a smile as he assured her, "If I lost you too, I assure you, I would turn the world upside down looking for you."

Sheryl stared at him. He looked as though he were trying to inject humor —of all things— into the situation.

Well, excuse the hell out of me for failing to see the humor in the situation, she thought acidly.

"Sheriff Jackson will also be looking for me," she tossed out, gambling on the fact that since Tim had told her that he was the sheriff's son and introduced himself as Tim Jackson. She hoped to hell that the boy had the same last name as his dad.

The man before her seemed unfazed by the information, affecting no more than mild interest and idle curiosity. "How would you know Nathaniel? You're not a local," he added.

He seemed to be on first name basis with the sheriff, she realized, feeling her hope dash where she had expected that one mention of Sheriff Jackson and he would squirm away like the vermin he was. Instead, he looked as though he wanted to hang up his boots and sit down to converse about mutual acquaintances!

She looked away, feeling the aching loss of that hope of escape.

"You have a very readable and expressive face," he observed.

She glared, "And what does my face say now?"

He studied her as though giving the matter serious consideration. "You have nothing to fear from me, Sheryl."

"Really, Mikey? Could have fooled me," she said with a feminine growl as she nodded at her bindings.

Amused irritation sprang into his eyes and he asked, "What the hell would you call me Mikey for?"

She paused. Had Tim made a mistake? "Isn't that your name?"

His gaze hardened. "My name isn't Mikey. Never call me that."

Then he turned abruptly on one heel and strode away too busy himself by the fireplace.

Hmm, have I touched a nerve, she wondered, tilting her head to the side as she studied him. *All right, then, from now on, Mikey it is until he gets angry enough that he tosses me out on my rear himself!*

A more pressing need made its presence known and she seized the opportunity to say with only a little taunting lilt to her voice, "Listen, Mikey, I need to use the restroom."

He didn't lift his head, kept fiddling with whatever he was doing.

The pressure increased. She really did need to go. She injected a little humility into her tone. "I need to use the restroom, Mike."

Nothing.

"Fine, what the hell should I call you?" she grated.

He lifted his head at once, masculine triumph glinting in his golden eyes, "Michael will do."

"*Michael,* I need the restroom, *now.*"

"No," he said shortly and went right back to his task.

Sheryl sputtered in disbelief. *Is he really that petty that he would put me through all the stress of getting his name right, only to say no? And to the call of nature? What kind of jerk kidnaps a woman and doesn't let her enjoy the simple pleasures of life; you know, pleasures like an empty bladder?*

"Why the hell not?" she demanded,

"If you think I'm gonna let you escape on my watch—" he began.

"Well, newsflash, big guy, you kidnapped a real flesh and blood woman with a working bladder. If you didn't want to have to deal with the nastiness of going to the loo, you should have kidnapped yourself a life-sized doll!"

As soon as the last two words escaped her lips, her words screeched to a halt and she paled. Life-sized doll? She knew very well what most men did with a life-sized doll these days and her throat worked as she swallowed a sudden knot of fear, staring at his bent head in sheer terror.

He lifted his head just then and looked back at her. Mutual understanding arched between them and then irritation slashed across his masculine features as he flung down the log of wood in his hand and climbed to his feet, positively bristling with what seemed a lot like righteous indignation.

"I am not so hard up for a woman that I would have to kidnap one or get a doll, so get your mind out of the gutter."

He was so disgusted at the train of thought she'd had that she felt instant relief. He wasn't going to try *that* then. "Well, then why are you holding me hostage? Money?"

He walked right up to her, and she became so aware of his huge size and his smooth, half-naked skin mere inches away.

As he leaned toward her, she started to shrink back until she realized he was reaching for the ropes around her wrist.

She watched in shock as he started to untie her.

"What do you want from me?" she prodded. "I can't give you money if I'm trussed up like Thanksgiving turkey in some cabin in the woods."

His gaze met hers briefly and then his humor returned as his eyes sparkled at her, "No, I don't imagine you can."

He loosened the ropes on her legs and stretched out a hand to help her to her feet, brimming with such gentlemanly courtesy that she felt her heart thud in her chest.

With stubborn defiance, she ignored the outstretched hand and got up on her own. Her legs promptly protested the sudden rush of blood with an intense sensation of pins and needles. She cried out and started to fall when Michael grabbed her and hauled her flush against his hard masculine chest.

All the breath whooshed out of Sheryl, and her hands, of their own accord, also came up and slammed against his chest.

Her eyes were twin saucers of shock as she stared up into his. He was hard, firm and muscular in all the right places, and being pressed against him from breast to waist was doing a number on her sanity. Her gaze fell on his lips just a centimeter or so away from hers, and she felt a shocking and absolutely unwanted flash of that unnamable feeling she'd had when she noticed him at the gas station for the first time.

Shakily, she shoved at his chest to extricate herself from the situation. He released her at once and stepped back.

She quirked an eyebrow in classic imitation of her sister, Kate. "The restroom?"

He pointed toward a small door in the corner, "Through there."

As she turned to head in that direction, he grabbed her

arm, forcing her to halt and risk one more glance at his harsh features. "I know you're thinking of escaping. Don't. I'm doing this for you."

Sheryl stared at him in mute disbelief, unable to wrap her mind around how he had conjured up the unmitigated gall to say such nonsense to her. Either he was very sick or very manipulative or truly evil. He had kidnapped her for her own good, had he?

Without stopping to think about it, she let fly with the flat of her palm and felt a spurt of wicked satisfaction as her palm crashed against his cheek. The force of the slap snapped his head back, but he gave no indication that it had even happened. He just regarded her in stoic silence for a few heartbeats until she felt like a heel and felt very small indeed beneath the force of that calm, steady regard.

Drawing herself up to her full height, she enunciated, "I don't know who the hell you think you are, Michael No-Surname, but don't you dare insult my intelligence and expect me to stand for it."

With that, she stamped into the restroom and slammed the door into place almost running in her haste to not let her emotions show in front of him. Then she turned on the tap to prevent him from hearing anything and she let herself slide to the floor in an almost boneless heap of despair.

Then she let the tears come.

CHAPTER 4

*M*ichael felt like a jerk.

He couldn't recall a time in living memory when a woman had shed tears because of him. In truth, not even Hannah, his childhood sweetheart and recent ex, had ever had cause to shed tears because of him. Now, listening to Sheryl's soft weeping behind the door, he felt each tear like a whiplash, and it was all he could do not to tear down the door and gather her up in his arms. He wanted to assure her she could slap him to her heart's content, and he wanted to dry the tears he knew would be on her soft cheeks. He wanted to kiss her until she either got angry all over again, or got pliant with need; either way, she wouldn't be crying anymore.

She had turned on the tap to prevent him from hearing anything but what she hadn't realized was that he was a shifter, which meant his hearing, like all his other senses, was somewhat more heightened than that of humans. He sighed, folding his arms across his chest as he listened to her tears.

In all fairness, I can't blame her. If I were a woman and a strange man kidnapped me and wouldn't say why, I might have dissolved in tears too. Heck, she has stayed strong for so long, she deserves a medal.

And that was one of the many things he liked about her. The woman had spunk. He listened again and heard her moving around. He could sense her inner turmoil and the spark of rebellion growing inside of her.

He sighed as he walked toward the front door, grabbing a shirt as he went and tugging it on. He let himself out, anticipating her next move. He couldn't read minds like Darryl could, but years of being able to calm people's emotions and make them feel what he wanted them to feel had made him more attuned to people's senses on an instinctive level rather than ability-based level. It had also made him very wary of using his abilities unless he absolutely had to because he hated to feel as though he was manipulating people's feelings. He didn't know her on a personal level, but he was willing to bet that she was even now plotting her escape through the single high window at the back of the restroom. That escape route was difficult and dangerous, but he had seen a determined glint in her eyes a few times that told him Sheryl Quinn was no wilting flower. She was a strong woman, and she would do what needed to be done.

Except, I will not let her, he thought as he planted himself at the back of the cabin, just out of her line of sight should she peek out the window before attempting her escape.

Sure enough, a slim jean-clad leg soon poked out the window, followed by its twin. His mouth quivered in amusement as he watched her shimmy halfway out the window with the effortless grace of an athlete, before sort of propelling herself and landing on all fours on the soft earth.

Michael let her land and glory in her 'escape' for a nanosecond before he drawled, "Took you long enough."

Sheryl spun around to look at him but to her credit, she

didn't scream or put on any fake apology. He could tell he had caught her off-guard though.

He continued as though they were merely two people who had an appointment, "I was almost afraid I was going to take root and start growing before you got the gumption to use the window."

She climbed to her full height and faced him, her lower chin jutting out in that stubbornness he was fast becoming accustomed to. "I'm leaving. And I *dare* you to try to stop me," she added, looking around wildly.

Her gaze lit on a long, fat stick and she grabbed it, hefting it with both hands like a club.

She looked adorable, he mused. Like a six-year-old fending off a great big Bear with a small piece of wood. At least she wasn't crying anymore, he thought. He preferred her rebellious and defiant any day over weeping and hurt.

He kept his hands at his side in a non-threatening gesture as he walked toward her, "I know you don't understand any of this, but I assure you, right now, this is the safest place in the world for you. I would never hurt you."

"You *kidnapped* me! That doesn't spell hurting me in your book?" she gasped, disbelief stamped onto her features.

Michael was fast developing a lively dislike for that word. Sure, he had taken her somewhere she didn't know against her will, but he was one of the good guys. He had only done it to protect her. Every time she harped on it, he felt bad and helpless all at once. He couldn't very well tell her that he had kidnapped her to protect her from a horde of murderous vampires. Aside from disbelieving him, she would laugh him into a mental asylum if he tried.

"Stay here, Sheryl. You're safe here," he told her, sincerity blazing from his eyes as he tried to tell her, without words, what he wanted to say. This *was* the safest place in the world for her right now, what with so many vampires passing her scent around.

Her upper lip curled in contempt and then, without another word, she turned and ran. Michael watched her go, standing perfectly still as she took several steps to take her far from him, while turning around to check that he wasn't pursuing her as she ran.

There's no other way; I'll have to scare her into trusting me, he thought.

Once she was out of sight, he let his transformation begin. His smooth skin gave way to thick, clean fur and his long legs became shorter but sturdier as they became Wolf legs. His hands shortened and curved until he was on all fours and his head elongated forward into his canine form. He grunted a little as he morphed into his shifter Wolf, his animal side exulting in the freedom of roaming the woods at last. Then he ran after her, taking a wide, roundabout road. He knew the woods like the back of his hand. He leaped with fluid grace, over several dead trees lining the forest floor, his long Wolf legs easily eating the distance as he went. His senses strained to search for peripheral signs of life or danger in the vicinity as he went. Everywhere was still, with the smell of dead dried leaves assailing his nostrils. Less than two seconds later, he was planted on the path he knew Sheryl was heading toward. He tried to look as nonchalant as any self-respecting ravenous Wolf possibly could as he nosed at dead tree branches, pretending to search for food.

Sheryl burst into the clearing where he was just then, and his eyes gleamed in triumph. He straightened, lifting his Wolf head and looking straight at her.

Sheryl stopped in her tracks, her expression frozen with fear as she stared back at him. A spurt of compassion stirred within Michael at the fact that he had to scare her, but he stayed the course, silencing his conscience. If she was scared and alive in his captivity, it was better than having her confident and dead at the hands of vampires.

Michael tossed his head and lifted his upper lip, showing a row of sharp, shiny white teeth as he threw back his head and bayed.

She screamed as though her vocal cords had only just recovered enough from the shock of his appearance to start working. Then she turned around and began running back the way she had come, even faster than she had when she had escaped from him earlier. Michael took a few running steps after her still in his Wolf form, and she screamed all the louder and increased her speed. She hit her foot against a branch in her path and fell over.

He skid to an immediate halt, afraid she had gotten hurt. But she was up again in a matter of a mere second, running for dear life.

He took a roundabout route as before, running as fast as he could, using his supernatural abilities. He arrived his former position, morphed back into his human form and was already running toward the sound of her screaming when she appeared, still running. She screamed again in stark terror when she saw him and launched herself straight into his arms, panting for breath.

"What?" he demanded, infusing urgency into his voice as he looked behind her as though checking for what had frightened her. "What is it?"

She pointed a shaky hand back the way she had come, her chest heaving with each breath.

Something about the almost wild look in her eyes warned him and he shook her slightly, trying to get her to calm down. She was on the verge of hysteria. "Use your words," he encouraged.

"Wolf," she panted. "Wolf," she repeated, turning around to face him. And then, before he could try to calm her with his ability to dictate emotions, she fainted dead away in his arms.

Michael felt like kicking himself. In the space of a mere two days since he had met Sheryl, she had fallen unconscious twice, and both times had been his fault.

He gathered her up in his arms and carried her indoors, letting her stillness be his penance. He laid her gently onto the mattress and fetched some cool water in a bowl. He picked a clean face towel from among his things and carried it over to her. He dipped the face towel into the bowl of water and wrung it out. Then he placed it over her face with great care. She gasped as the cool towel touched her skin, and her eyes fell open.

He repeated the motion, and she gave a small *brrr*. "It's cold, you dolt."

He grinned, unable to help himself. She was pure dynamite. "I know it's cold. I never heard of anyone being revived with warm water. Besides, if you're cold, it's your own fault. I wasn't the one who took off, running in the woods while wearing nothing more than a skinny pair of jeans and a tiny little insignificant crop top."

She gave him a dirty look even as her stomach rumbled loudly.

"Are you hungry?" he asked.

"What do you think?" she grumbled. Her stomach rumbled some more. "I had been on the road all day yesterday, and apart from some hurriedly eaten hamburger, *someone* somehow got me unconscious and dragged me off into the night before I'd had a chance for a proper meal. How *did* you get me here?" she demanded.

He deserved that for asking, he thought with an inward sigh as he ignored her and went and grabbed a plate of fried eggs and a few slices of bread for her.

She was distracted at once from her last line of questioning, just as he had hoped. She peeked at the plate, her eyes assessing the contents, then she looked up at him, "Funny you didn't think to ask if I was vegetarian."

Panic shot through him. He had driven to the first store he found and packed as many things as his hands could grab after he had knocked her out; mostly food things. And that now he thought about it, they *weren't* vegetarian diets.

Kidnapping her to save her life had seemed gallant and necessary. But now, in hindsight, and given all the grief she had given him, he was sorely beginning to question the wisdom of that idea.

"Are you vegetarian?" he asked, already knowing the answer would be a cheeky yes.

She didn't answer though. Just gave him a look that spoke volumes. He cursed under his breath.

She cocked one eyebrow, "Jeez. Talk about intolerance. What have you got against vegetarians?"

He sighed, scrubbing a hand down his face. "No. No. I swear, it's not that. It's cool. It's just… I don't have vegetarian stuff here. Apart from a few grains and veggies that is. I packed chicken, ham, eggs, sausages and stuff like that. A few crackers too."

She lifted one shoulder in a negligent shrug, "Well, pardon me for inconveniencing my kidnapper."

"Could you stop calling me that?" he demanded.

She rolled her eyes. "It's what you are. Do you have my phone?" she asked in the next breath.

He grabbed some mangoes, apples and a few cherries, thrust them onto a plate and waved them in front of her nose.

She looked at the offering with something approaching mild interest on her vivid features, then with a small dismissive nod, she motioned for him to drop it onto the bedside table.

Great. Now, he got to wait on her hand and foot. He did as she had indicated, and with a satisfied sigh, she adjusted her pillows until she could lean back against them in a semi-sitting position.

"By the way, I'm not vegetarian. But serves you right for assuming I wasn't," she added, her eyes gleaming with satisfaction.

He bit back a grin. Sheryl looked so pleased with herself just now that he couldn't help remembering Theodore's little girl, Carla, when she was being especially mischievous.

"So, future kidnapping tips, according to you: don't assume the culinary habits of the kidnappee?"

Sheryl laughed, "I've never heard that word, but yeah, you get my drift."

She adjusted her buttocks to get more comfortable and then she picked one cherry and carried it to her lips. Watching her soft pink lips curl around the fleshy fruit with a moan of gastronomic pleasure made him suddenly picture those same lips curled around the velvety tip of his dick.

The top of his head almost came off. He got hard fast. Very fast. His Wolf was tearing away at his insides, demanding to be free. His nostrils flared as his Wolf picked up her sweet feminine scent and his senses reacted. He wanted her very badly. As though she could hear his thoughts, the damn woman chose that exact moment to lick her lips and make a small sound in the back of her throat like a moan. His dick pressed with more insistence against his fly and his Wolf growled as he strove for control.

Hurriedly, he spun on his heel and stalked off, back toward the safety of the fireplace as he busied himself once more with setting a roaring fire going. As he worked, Michael tried to understand what exactly was going on. He had never had a problem getting along with women, but he certainly wasn't the sort of man who walked around with a constant hard-on. What was happening to him? Ever since Sheryl Quinn crashed into his life, he had been hard, and it was getting uncomfortable. If he hadn't moved so fast just now, he wouldn't have been able to stop her from seeing his arousal. And he wasn't a fool; he knew he had her at a disadvantage with the whole kidnapping deal. So, if she saw his arousal, she would rightly feel threatened and afraid, and that was the last thing he wanted. His Wolf stirred. He couldn't bear for her to think of him as some sort of monster; although, why it should matter so very much what she thought of him was a topic he didn't want to examine too closely.

Besides, it might very well make her more determined to escape his clutches and she would only fall right into Roy's arms. And he would never be able to forgive or live with himself if that happened.

"I still need my phone please," Sheryl called from behind him.

"I didn't see a phone when I picked you up," he told her.

"But my sister… Listen, maybe I left it in my bedroom at the hotel then, but the thing is, I need to speak to Kate soon, otherwise, she would be all over my disappearance. And you don't want that."

He needed to give Connor some feedback, he thought with a muttered curse as his gaze landed on his own phone. He hadn't called to inform him of his change of plans or what he had learned about Roy's ring and his plans.

If he hadn't been so distracted by Sheryl…

He threw Sheryl a glance. She had finished eating. He got up and grabbed her hands and tied them again as securely as he had before while she fumed in silence.

Then he grabbed his phone and went outside to make a call; he didn't want her listening in.

"Where in the blue blazes have you been since last night? I

was gonna crash Roy's place with guns blazing," Connor grated down the line as soon as he received the call.

Michael sighed. He had wanted to avoid Connor yelling; seemed he was too late for that. Keeping his voice down, he narrated most of what had happened to Connor but for some reason he didn't mention Sheryl or what had transpired. It seemed somewhat … personal and private.

When he was done, Connor growled, "That's great work you did, son. So, the ring is the charm, eh? Well, get your ass over here pronto. We've got work to do finding out what makes that ring work."

Michael cast a glance back at the silent cabin behind him. It was situated high in the mountains very far from town. He couldn't very well dash back into Angel Springs nor did he want to because it would mean leaving her alone and she could get up to all sorts of mischief that made his hair stand on end just imagining it. Plus, the vampires could discover her location through him. If he walked back into town someone was bound to see and try to trail him.

"I have, uh… something of a situation here," Michael began.

"A situation? Where exactly are you?" Connor demanded.

"I can't say where I am right now. I'm gonna tell you as soon as it's sorted out. But right now, you're gonna have to take point on finding out what Roy wants to do next."

"You're not in any trouble, are you?" Connor asked.

Memories of his constant arousal anytime Sheryl was near intruded, and Michael sighed, "That remains to be seen."

Silence reigned a bit on the line then Connor said quietly, "Well, I trust you, man. I always have, always will. Whatever it is that you need to do, deal with it as fast as you can and get back here."

"Okay."

"And listen," Connor continued just as Michael was about

to hang up. "Don't try to do anything dangerous alone. If you get in trouble, just call and I and the others will be there in a flash."

Being cooped up with a certain curly-headed brunette was some dangerous shit but he could hardly ask for help with that since he had brought it upon himself.

Is that the only reason? His Wolf sniggered. *Or do you just want her all to yourself?*

He was just glad he wasn't speaking to Darryl, Michael thought as he gave a grunt of assent and hung up as fast as he could. Darryl would have picked the information right off his mind even over the phone line.

He trudged back up to the cabin, unwilling to admit his footsteps were a bit faster than they needed to be, unwilling to admit that his hands were shaky or that he was feeling a definite need to gaze into Sheryl's perfectly ordinary brown eyes again for reasons he didn't dare explain to himself, unwilling to admit that the small smile curving his lips was from anticipation of one of her sarcastic comebacks.

He threw open the front door, still smiling, but his smile vanished at the sight in front of him: Sheryl had somehow freed herself and she was now sitting on a cushion a few feet away with a loaded shotgun pointed right at his head.

CHAPTER 5

"Keep your hands above your head," Sheryl purred, finger on the trigger to show she meant business. "Keep 'em right where I can see them."

Michael stared at her in mute fascination, his expression seeming as though he thought she were the eighth wonder of the world, but he didn't move a muscle either to obey her or threaten her.

She raised the gun higher as she barked, "Hands. Now!"

He slowly lifted his hands on either side of his head. Her eyes scanned his rugged features, and she felt a flash of irritation because he didn't look the least bit scared. Instead, he looked as breezy and handsome as though he were posing for the centerspread of GQ.

"Hands are up," he informed her in a calm tone that chaffed.

She motioned with the gun for him to move to the side. He obeyed slowly, his gaze locked on hers. He wasn't even sparing the gun a second glance; almost as though he didn't think it could harm him.

"You're not really gonna shoot me," he declared.

Sheryl promptly shot the small throw pillow on the floor a few inches from his feet. He looked at it and back at her, and an indefinable flash of something passed in his strange colored eyes.

Well, she wasn't interested in examining what it was. She wanted out of this jungle and he was her ticket to getting out.

"Throw your phone to me," she ordered.

He slowly reached into his pocket and drew out the phone with his right hand. Sheryl's hungry gaze was fastened on the phone. If she got it, she could call for help and get someone to track the number and she could be out of here in a flash. Thank goodness.

"Hurry up," she snapped when he seemed to hesitate.

"And if I don't?" he demanded in that calm cultured voice of his.

A flash of irrational fear coursed through her and she hefted the shotgun, letting the motion speak for her.

Michael's gaze scanned her face as though looking for something.

She schooled her features to be unreadable.

His gaze locked on hers, he slowly held up the phone with his right hand. Sheryl tensed to catch it when he threw it. Rather than throw it though, he squeezed until it shattered into several tiny pieces. Then he let the pieces fall to the ground beside his booted feet.

Sheryl's disbelieving gaze drifted over the shattered pieces of the phone as she fought down the urge to burst into tears of frustration. That phone had been her ticket out of here, and he had ruined it.

Tears filled her eyes as she looked at the pieces then she raised wounded, broken eyes to his, wondering what to do. She knew she could never shoot a man in cold blood; she had only been bluffing. But she hadn't expected him to call her bluff so cruelly. She tried to rise from her seated position, still seething, when pain in her ankle made her cry out and she sat back down at once.

Concern wreathed Michael's face, and he was beside her in a flash, moving so fast he was almost a blur. "Are you all right?"

She could see genuine concern in his features, but it did nothing to endear him to her after he had so callously destroyed her only hope of making a phone call and leaving the jungle.

She fisted a hand in his shirtfront, her expression pleading, "Please. Let me go. I can't stay here."

He was silent for a moment, his gaze focused on her ankle as he examined the sprain. Then he replied, "When did you sprain your ankle? Why didn't you tell me you were in pain?"

Sheryl felt like shaking him. A sprained ankle was the least of her worries. Anger made her voice a bit waspish as she responded, "I fell trying to get away from that Wolf earlier."

He looked as though he had been flogged. "I'm sorry," he murmured, contrite as though it were his fault.

She supposed in a way it *was* his fault. If he hadn't grabbed her from her hotel, she wouldn't be in this mess now and she certainly wouldn't have hurt herself either.

"You don't get off that easily Michael. What you're doing is a crime. Let me get out of here. I swear I won't call the cops," she added. "I won't tell anyone."

He lifted his eyes to hers, sincerity blazing out of them with such intensity that her breath caught in her throat, "I want to let you go. I just don't see how I can do that."

She frowned at him, trying to understand as he sprang to his feet and began to pace.

"What aren't you telling me," she demanded, suddenly certain there was something he was shielding from her. She grabbed his arm as he came within reach and gave him an urgent shake. "How am I mixed up in all of this?"

"You tell me," he countered. "I saw you spying on those men. What did you hope to find out?"

She shrugged, "They seemed like a shady sort. I was just doing my bit to secure my environment. I mean, did you see that diamond sword? They had to have been smugglers, or worse."

"Worse," he assured her without cracking a smile.

Her eyes rounded at the severity of his tone and her face turned a deathly shade of grey. He broke her gaze for a minute, heaving a put-upon sigh. He acted as though she had made him feel like a heel for diming the animation in her face or something. *But he has to let me know if I am in danger; it's the only way to guarantee my cooperation and safety. He can't expect me to just go along with it. I have to know what this is all about.*

He turned to face her then. His eyes were now such a dark gold color, they were mesmerizing. "Some men are after you Sheryl. That's the only reason I took you. I swear it was the only way to keep you safe and out of their reach until all this blows over."

Blood drained from her face some more. "Why would anyone be after me?"

"Those men you were spying on? They saw you, and they're searching for you," he told her. "And they're not smugglers."

Her eyes narrowed in suspicion. She badly wanted to ask what they were if they weren't smugglers, but her guts failed her. She didn't think she was ready to know just what.

"Well, I saw you talking to the same men by the pool, and you all seemed pretty chummy. How do I know you aren't all working together to keep me out of the way just long enough for you to complete whatever evil plan you were hatching?"

Disgust flashed across his features, "I'm nothing like those men. I am *not* working with them."

Sheryl read sincerity in his gaze but her memory of her poor results with reading Sloan was still too fresh. She didn't trust herself when it came to reading men and deciphering their honesty.

As though he had read the distrust in her mind, Michael fell silent. He turned away and got something from a cupboard. She saw at once that it was an ointment and she reached out to take it from him. But he ignored her outstretched hand and gently picked up her foot and placed it onto his laps.

Sheryl froze in disbelief as he began to apply the ointment onto her ankle. His touch was feather-light, almost a caress as he stroked his finger in repetitive rhythms over her skin. Tendrils of sensation flowed up her leg from her ankle as he touched her and she shifted in delightful discomfort, feeling an undeniable rush of pleasure pool at the juncture of her thighs. Everything about this man affected her beyond words; he made her want to be wild and wanton and pliant and utterly female in his arms all at once. One look into his smoldering eyes and in spite of herself, she could feel her entire being responding to his raw heat and naked sex appeal. His hard brawny muscles made her feel very petite and feminine in comparison. His clean masculine scent made her think of burying her nose in his skin and inhaling deeply.

Unable to help herself, she reached out one hand and stroked his hand. He froze, his gaze jerking up to hers as something wild and animal moved in the depths of his gaze. Sheryl jerked her hand back in reaction. He returned his gaze to his ministrations and her hand once more started to reach for him of its own volition. Tightening the offending hand into a fist, she jerked it back to her side.

Unwise, she chided herself. *I have yet to vet his story; to ascertain his identity; to be certain he isn't mixed up in something illegal and dangerous with those other men. I can't afford to feel anything for him beyond contempt.*

But she couldn't deny that deep feminine intuition that told her she was… well, safe with him. Somehow, he didn't strike her as the sort of man she had something to fear from. Sure, he had this element of danger he wore about him like a cloak but that just added to his air of mystery. It didn't seem…sinister.

The ointment was instantly absorbed by her skin, but he didn't release her yet. His hands were still stroking her ankle. Sheryl could feel herself reacting against her will to his touch; her nipples hardened into small points beneath her bra. A small moan escaped her throat unbidden, and his gaze jerked up to hers. There it was again, that wild animal thing in the depths of his eyes.

Her breath caught in her throat at the answering heat in his gaze and she moaned again. His eyes dropped to her lips and lifted again to hers. She saw him swallow, his Adam's apple bobbing.

"What?" he demanded, desire and lust making his voice harsh.

Sheryl shook her head, "Nothing."

His hand was still caressing her ankle and she was still feeling shivers of desire trembling up her skin.

"I'm fine now," she insisted making her voice hard.

He lifted her leg off his lap and returned it to the floor before taking his hands off her ankle.

The motion drew her eyes to the juncture of his thighs and the unmistakable bulge beneath his pants made her breath catch in her throat again. He wanted her just as much as she wanted him.

She couldn't be sure which of them made a move or signal but one minute they were both breathing hard and fighting a losing battle for control, then the next minute they were both entwined with each other on the bed.

They came together in a flash, his tongue probing into her mouth with bold strokes, kissing, caressing, melding, teasing until she was a quivering mass of need and want. His hands cupped her ass, holding her up against him while he pressed himself against the juncture of her thighs.

Sheryl moaned again, her hands encircling his neck and holding him close as they made love to each other with their mouths.

Michael let his lips trail down the side of her neck, his tongue poked out a little to lave at her collarbone, and then his lips drifted once more back up to hers.

"You're so sweet," he moaned. "So very sweet."

He shoved up her crop top, exposing one naked breast to his hands and he groaned when he saw her round soft breasts. "So fucking hot."

He bent his head at once, and took her nipple in his mouth, groaning with masculine pleasure as he began to suck her. His other hand covered her other breast, and he began to gently knead the soft skin.

"You taste amazing," he whispered. His voice didn't sound quite like his; it seemed to have an almost animal quality beneath it. It came out more like a growl but somehow, she understood him at an almost instinctive level.

Sheryl was so wet she almost couldn't stand it. She wanted him to touch her deep inside where she was so wet, but her pants were getting in the way. Unable to wait, she shoved her right hand down the front of her pants and straight into her panties. She was so fucking wet!

"I'm so wet! So wet for you," she moaned as she began to finger herself even as he sucked her breast. It had been so long since she felt this level of wild abandon, she thought twisting her waist.

Michael lifted his head from her breast, his eyes gleaming as he watched her stroke herself through her pants. "Let me taste you," he whispered.

Sheryl brought her hand out of her panties and showed it to him. It was dripping with vaginal juices and his eyes became even hotter as soon as he saw it. He caught her wrist and carried the hand to his mouth, taking first one finger and then the next in his mouth in tantalizing, slow strokes. He moaned.

"Delicious," he whispered as he continued to suck all her fingers deeply, licking off all the vaginal juices on each one. "Give me more," he ordered.

She dipped her hand again beneath her pants and brought it out coated with more juices. His tender strokes and sensuous touches were making her almost cum, she thought, watching as he sucked her fingers and tasted her.

I want that bold tongue laving at my pussy, Sheryl thought squirming. *I want him with a keening desperation that would probably have frightened me in saner moments. But right now, I can't think. Right now, all I want is him; just him.*

Michael leaned forward and took her lips in another tantalizing kiss, making her taste herself on his lips.

Sheryl wrapped one leg around his waist and in her excitement forgot her injury on the other ankle as she made to lift that leg too. Pain speared through her and she cried out in reaction.

Michael wrenched himself away at once, his eyes wide and contrite, "Oh shit. Did I hurt you?" he demanded with an urgency underlined with concern. "What did I do?"

She shook her head as the pain began to recede. "I just forgot to go easy on that ankle, is all. I'll be fine."

Suddenly she was shy and couldn't meet his eyes. What had possessed her to kiss him like that and let him kiss her like that? She had behaved with such wild abandon in his arms. They were two total strangers who didn't even know each other and if he hadn't kidnapped her, he wouldn't even be a blip on her radar. Yet even now she wanted him with an intensity that defied all logic. Sometimes it seemed that all he had to do was look at her and she lost all control.

Fine, she didn't want any lasting commitment, but she sure wanted a taste of him. He was devastatingly handsome and very masculine. She wanted him to make love to her even if it was just once with no strings attached. There, she had finally admitted it to herself, she thought, feeling very liberated at the thought.

Stockholm Syndrome, her subconscious ruled.

Shut it, she scolded her inner voice.

She started to lift her head to ask him to touch her again, but his deep voice overrode hers before she could get a word out.

"I'm sorry. This should never have happened. I uh, took advantage of you, didn't I? I am so very sorry, Sheryl, and I assure you, I regret my actions and detest what I just did. It won't happen again," he told her.

Sheryl stared, feeling as though she had been slapped. "I don't understand."

Michael shrugged, "I kidnapped you, Sheryl. This isn't an ideal situation. I shouldn't have put my hands on you just now. I had no right."

"I wasn't complaining," she pointed out, frustrated desire rising and creating an unwelcome form of sexual tension in her.

"Of course, you weren't. How could you? Maybe you felt you *couldn't* complain but I swear if I ever try it again, you're welcome to slap my face."

She did want to slap his face but not for the reason he thought. He made her sound like some witless bimbo who couldn't protect herself or who didn't know what she wanted. She had wanted him to put his hands and tongue and dick in her and all over her. She had wanted him to suck her breasts and her pussy. She had wanted him to kiss and caress her. She had wanted his hands all over her. She had wanted him, period. Ever since she had clapped eyes on him at the gas station, she had wanted him, but she had been denying it to herself. There was no sense denying it now was there? She had decided she wanted him in her bed no strings attached, and he had had the effrontery and the unmitigated gall to suggest that she was some mindless person who would let him have his way with her if that wasn't what she wanted as if she didn't know her own mind.

She met his gaze, letting him see the absolute loathing in her eyes as she said, "I'm glad you've realized your mistake. Make it up to me by letting me get out of here right now."

He sighed, his gaze dropping to her ankle, "You need to rest that leg. Even if by some chance I was foolish enough to consider letting you go, you're in no shape to escape if those guys found you."

"That's my own problem not yours," she pointed out. "I didn't ask you to play Sir Galahad," she spat in frustration.

He turned and began to head for the front door.

"Don't you dare walk away Michael, I need to get out of here today," she thundered.

"Don't be such a shrew," he chided.

"Shrew?" she sputtered. "You kidnapped me and yanked me off on some journey I am in no way interested in and you think I'm a shrew? I should be on the first leg of my trip to Arizona now and here I am stuck in a cabin with you, and you have the gall to criticize my manners?"

"Well, when you put it that way—" he began with a half grin.

"Cut it out! I'm serious," she yelled.

His expression was schooled into one of aloof neutrality

as he towered over her. "Listen up. You're gonna be here for some days and that's that. Get used to it."

With a muffled oath, she flung her shoe at him, but he had already shut the door behind him, so her missile missed him entirely and thumped with annoying impotence against the closed door.

CHAPTER 6

"We need to move fast," Roy Davison announced, tossing a death glare at his men.

Sean, his right-hand man, nodded and began to lift more of the nails and construction materials onto the flatbed of the truck in the yard just outside Roy's strange warehouse.

Roy had moved his men from the caves where they had made their headquarters to a house just outside Angel Springs and now, he felt the need to move again. Something about that girl with the scrunchy who had been spying on him and the other vampires bothered him. He didn't like to take chances. It was true she had shut down Michael Bennet when he had tried to approach her, but if there was something Roy knew about the Exotic Pack, it was that they were ladies' men; every last one of them. No woman really withstood their charms for long. If Michael had taken a liking to that woman, it was only a matter of time before she caved in to his attentions. And if she had heard more than she should … then it was only a matter of time until the Exotic boys were beating down his door.

No! My secrets will not *become the subject of pillow talk,* he thought with vicious anger. *I will not allow that woman to live long enough to share whatever she had heard with anyone. Except, I have to find her first,* he thought pinching the bridge of his nose in anger. *I have staked out her room since that night and haven't seen any sign of her. For that matter, I haven't seen any sign of Michael Bennet around town either,* he thought, feeling anger simmer beneath the surface at the thought of the Wolf shifter.

Just then, Sean ambled in, carrying a toolbox, and it clattered to the ground, spilling its contents onto the floor. He paled and threw Roy a glance as though expecting Roy to yell at him. When his master said nothing, Sean continued to pack up the contents.

Roy's hands fisted at his sides as he forced himself to keep still rather than taking over from the men and completing the task in a flash with his vampire abilities.

A loud horn blared as someone drove up and Roy lifted his head, his eyes widening in surprise as Connor Philips jumped out of the truck along with Darryl and Justin. Roy let his contempt show as he flicked a glance over the three shifters.

"Roy Corning," Connor hailed in greeting, striding up to the vampire and backslapping him as though they were old friends.

Roy Corning was Roy Davison to everyone who knew him, but the shifter brothers had discovered his real identity as the son of Atlas Corning and ever since then they had taken to calling him that name. Sometimes he thought they took a wicked delight in seeing his impatience at the realization that his carefully kept secret of the identity of his progenitor wasn't so secret anymore.

Roy knew he had gotten the ability to walk in the sun when he inherited his father's ring, but he always had to wear a cowboy hat to dim the glare and his skin was permanently red once he was under the sun giving people the impression that his face was suffused in angry red color.

Now though, the red color suffusing his face was real anger. He couldn't imagine any two people in the world he hated more than Connor Philips and Michael Bennet and he wasn't exactly thrilled to see Connor right here. He hadn't wanted the Exotic Pack to know about his new hideout and yet, as always, they seemed to be one step ahead of him. If he didn't know better, he would think they had a mole inside his team rather than the other way round, he thought, thinking gleefully of the faithful servant he had stashed away on the grounds of Exotic Rescue.

"Get those cursed hands off me," Roy grunted flinging away the offending hand.

Connor chuckled, "What? No greeting for me?"

Roy glared at the three men, "What do you want?"

All traces of humor were immediately wiped from Connor's face and he grabbed Roy by the collar and shook him, "Glad you asked, you sonofabitch."

Before Roy could guess his intent, Connor let fly with his fist and landed a solid punch straight into Roy's nose. Pain shot through Roy with inhuman intensity, and he cried out, fangs appearing as he returned the blow— or at least he tried to. Connor blocked it with humiliating ease.

"Ye gat no right ter be on my property," Roy yelled, his Texas twang making itself obvious now that he was so upset.

Connor showed him a wolfish grin, "Who's gonna stop me?"

The second punch almost removed a fang. Roy kneed Connor in the groin and the shifter promptly doubled over even as the other men and Sean were all knocked out by Darryl and Justin.

"I want to make sure you take a real good look at the man who's gonna stop you," Roy growled as he reached for

Connor again. This time though the shifter was waiting for him. He grabbed Roy's hand and twisted it until it made a loud pop.

Roy screamed. At the same time, he felt Connor twist the ring on his little finger off and he howled in outrage and pain even as the morning sun began to burn him.

With a yelp, Roy dove indoors and slammed the door shut behind him, quivering in pain and outrage, already red from head to toe with angry scorch marks all over his skin.

Connor laughed as he held the ring aloft, "Come on out here and get it, Roy. Damn that was almost too easy."

Roy ignored him, already stripping off his burning clothes and diving into his bathroom to soak himself in the tub. He threw in three shamrocks into the water and some herbs before entering and letting his skin begin to recover.

His mind worked furiously. Just as he had feared his secret had been revealed because why else would Connor and his men attack him and steal his ring? The ring had been the most useful thing he had gotten from his father and it had helped him walk in daytime. Now Connor had gone and collected it which meant the Pack knew all about his secret. But did they also know that their precious Tailan mineral was used in making the ring, he wondered.

That was the most closely guarded secret which he had revealed to no one, not even Lloyd and Gary. He was glad now that he had kept that information private because he wouldn't put it past the brothers to destroy the one mineral that could heal shifters if they found out that it also sustained him and gave him powers to walk in the daylight.

His instincts had been right then. That stupid bitch had overhead his plans with the other vampires and she had squealed like a pig to Michael.

Well, he would just have to take care of her then, he

thought grabbing his phone from its resting place beside the tub.

He dialed Gary's number from memory and spat into the phone, "I'm changing the instructions on that girl. Don't bother taking her in alive anymore. Kill her. Make it very slow and very painful."

He heard Gary's stupefied silence and he knew the other man was trying to reconcile this new order with the previous one to find her and bring her in alive.

"Sir I already told the other vampires—"

"Tell them the Vampire King changed the instructions," Roy spat curtly. And then he hung up, still fuming as his skin finally began to heal.

The brothers had set back his plans by taking that ring. It meant he couldn't move around until nightfall. But what they didn't know was that he had another ring; he just needed to wait for nightfall to go get it.

His thoughts churned as he considered the woman who had that second ring in her possession; she had been his father's concubine and she hated him as much as he hated her. He would just have to find a way to get it from her, he thought already feeling anticipation at their confrontation course through him.

* * *

MICHAEL KNEW HE SHOULDN'T GO INSIDE THE CABIN JUST YET. Sheryl was still mad at him several hours later; he could sense her emotions even from where he was by the side of the cabin. With a sigh, he leaned his head back against the trees and shut his eyes trying to understand how life could be so simple and yet so complicated.

He drifted off to sleep for a few minutes and jerked himself awake when an ant bit him. Now he was sleeping in the woods like some homeless hobo because he wanted to avoid Sheryl and the inevitable confrontation. She wasn't wrong for wanting to leave here but how could he really explain to her the extent of the danger she was in without her thinking he was either a wicked, manipulative man or a chronic liar. If he mentioned vampires, she would either laugh or kill him with her bare hands. And how could he tell her only part of the story without revealing the truth about himself? How could he tell her he was a shifter and not reveal the truth about the Pack and others? He couldn't endanger his brothers. What if she didn't understand? What if she spilled their secret to the wrong people?

He was almost feeling a headache coming on from trying to disentangle his tumultuous thoughts and feelings. Unbidden he recalled how he had touched Sheryl and her soft cries as he touched her and sucked her. He had wanted to make love to her right then and there when she had screamed, and he had been absolutely horrified at himself for taking advantage of her. His Wolf had been past caring. It had wanted satisfaction and all he had been able to think about was burying himself in her to the hilt. He wanted her with a desperation that defied all reason.

She had seemed very angry too; and he couldn't blame her.

He looked down at his hands. He couldn't keep her here anymore, he thought to himself. He had to let her go. Perhaps if she left town the vampires wouldn't be able to hurt her again, he thought.

His mind made up, he stood up and almost raced for the house in his eagerness to find her and tell her he could return her to town tomorrow so long as she left town at once. Her ankle seemed to have healed somewhat because he had heard her moving around.

The balm he had applied contained a very tiny trace of

Tailan and he knew it had quick healing properties. She should be fine by now since it was almost sundown.

With a sigh, he pushed open the door prepared to face her wrath. He drew up short when he saw the empty cabin waiting for him. Where was she?

Panic seared through him. He had been by the side of the cabin and he had listened to her movements. Had he slept off for longer than a few minutes then?

He opened up his supernatural senses trying to get a feel for where she was. The entire jungle was silent. Dusk was falling fast, and the skies seemed dark as though it was going to rain.

"Sheryl!" he screamed. His voice echoed back to him.

His heartbeat sped up in alarm. How could he find her? She could be in any manner of danger out there in the woods and there was nothing he could do about it until he could find her.

With a low growl, he changed into his Wolf form and bent to sniff the ground. His sharp Wolf sense of smell picked up her scent at once and, with relief, he set off in that direction just as the clouds opened up and it began to rain. Apparently, she had come out of the house and walked straight down the path into the bushes. He followed the trail, stepping softly but increasing his pace. He didn't want the rain to wash off her scent before he had a chance to find her. He heard the sound of weeping off in the bushes. Michael changed back into his human form just out of sight of Sheryl and hurried toward her.

Sheryl lifted her head as he came and she sniffed, her eyes red and wet even as she sat beneath the steadily pouring rain. Her hair was plastered to her face and her clothes were sodding wet; yet something about her was so very gorgeous and appealing. He felt like howling like Tarzan and staking his claim on her.

He knelt beside her, "Are you crying because I'm an idiot or because *you're* sitting in the rain like an idiot?"

She glared at him in angry silence.

He chuckled, feeling his heart lift with joy at that defiant look. At least he hadn't broken her spirits because he was being an absolute fool. "Let's get you back inside," he said.

She started crying again.

Michael stared in confusion. She was beside herself, weeping so profusely and noisily that he felt helpless. This was the second time he had made her cry. Something had to be wrong with him. Maybe he needed to stay away from her.

Slowly he cupped her face in his hands, forcing her to look at him and he stared straight into her eyes. In less than a minute, his powers enveloped her like a warm cocoon, and she started to quiet down. Her tears eased into tiny hiccups and she began to feel almost sleepy.

Pleased, he gathered her up in his arms and that was when he spotted the little makeshift walking stick lying on the ground.

"Boy, you were really determined to get away from me, weren't you?" he asked with a sad laugh as he kicked it.

She shrugged but said nothing.

With a sigh he turned back toward the cabin, more determined than ever to return her to her hotel room first thing tomorrow morning. *I'll take her out of town myself if it means she stops being so miserable around me,* he vowed. *But why do I get this hollow feeling in the pit of my stomach every time I think of her leaving?* he wondered.

He felt a deep growl pushing to escape. His wolf clearly was none to pleased with how he was handling things.

Michael grit his teeth as he did his best to ignore it. His wolf didn't understand things could be complicated…

Once they reached the cabin, Michael placed her gently onto the cushion and busied himself getting more logs into the fireplace. The weather was already chilly, and he was willing to bet she would want a warm bath.

"You need to dry off otherwise you would get a cold," he told her as he handed her a stack of clothes.

She eyed them warily, "Where did you get clothes from?"

He shrugged, "I picked them up the first day I... brought you here. They may not be your style, but I think they'll fit."

He felt his mouth go dry as he watched her examine the small tank top and the thigh-high shorts he had picked out for her. A flat soled knee-length boot was also part of the ensemble and as he looked at her, he couldn't help imagining her in those clothes. Her curves would be accentuated and beautifully displayed. Her soft, big ass would curve in a gentle arc that just begged for a man to stroke it, her beautiful breasts would bounce, big and free beneath the pretty lace of the white tank top. He was already getting an erection, he thought, forcing his thoughts away from the dangerous path they had taken. He could already feel his Wolf stirring in interest as animal lust and wild, unbridled passion rent him. He squeezed his hands into tight fists, fighting for control.

Sheryl nodded her thanks and acceptance of the clothes as she rose to her feet, limping just a little. He was pleased to see that the ointment had taken effect.

"Feel better?" he asked as he watched her head for the bathroom.

She nodded.

Michael shoved a hand through his hair in frustration. He never would have pegged her for the sort to deal him the silent treatment and it was starting to grate on his nerves. "Say something damnit."

She faced him, her eyes twin pools of indescribable emotions.

"It doesn't matter what I say Michael. You do what you

want," she told him in a forlorn voice as though she had given up or something.

Her tone scared him. He had heard that exact same tone before, he thought, alarm skittering along his nerve endings as memory struck. This was the same tone his last partner in the Secret Ops, Eddie, had used right before they found him dead. Eddie had gotten depressed and lost all will to live and gotten so careless while they were on duty that he had been killed.

He straightened as he looked at her. He hadn't been able to protect Eddie or forgive himself since then. He was damned if he would let Sheryl become careless and fall into Roy's hands because she was depressed or upset with him. "Tell me what you want. Anything," he added as though it were a vow.

"I want to go home," she announced.

"Done," he agreed at once.

He saw the surprise and suspicion flicker in her liquid brown eyes, and he nodded to show he was serious, "First thing tomorrow morning you're getting out of here. I swear it."

He let her see the sincerity in his gaze and then some. She stared at him some more as though unable to believe it. Then with a wry nod of her own, she turned and headed into the bathroom. He knew the tap in the cabin didn't produce hot water, so he handed her a bucket of warm water.

She took it without a word; but she did pause to search his eyes. He didn't know what she was looking for or whether she found it, but she seemed to look at him now with the kind of interest women showed around a man they liked. She was no more looking at him like the Big Bad Wolf in her story. She was looking at him as though she wanted him. He frowned, not daring to trust his eyes. He knew he wanted her, but he couldn't blame her for not reciprocating.

After all, he *had* kidnapped her and whisked her away from all that was dear and familiar.

She bit her lip just then, and his Wolf growled within him, lust hitting him like a kick in the stomach. She was delectable. She was enchanting. She was sexy as hell. Her eyes sparkled with a delightful combination of come-hither and sexy kitten vibes, and he swallowed a strangled groan. Maybe she didn't even know how she was looking at him or what that look could do to a man. For all her astonishing beauty and poise, there was this air of innocence that clung to her.

As though she had read his thoughts, she gave him a glinting half-smile and then she slammed the door in his face.

With a sigh, he returned to the fireplace and was adding more logs onto the fireplace when the bathroom door popped open again a few minutes later.

He didn't bother turning around as he asked, "Would you like a cup of hot tea? Something to warm you up a little more?"

Silence.

"Sheryl?" he prodded as he looked over his shoulder.

His next words died in his throat at the vision in front of his eyes. Sheryl was standing behind him, stark naked, her hands at either side of her hips, a soft smile playing about her lips. Her breasts were full and round pointing at a perfect ninety-degree angle, her skin looked as silky and soft as a baby's, her hair had been blow-dried to frame her face in gentle waves, her face was scrubbed clean and without makeup, yet entrancing. She was naked as the day she was born, and he had never seen a more attractive woman in his entire life.

It was the most erotic sight he had ever seen, and he came

to his feet, absolutely dumbfounded as he let his hungry gaze feast on her.

"Sheryl," he breathed again but this time the sound was more like a throaty whisper.

She tilted her head to one side, "You said I could have whatever I want Michael. Well, I've decided that I want you. Make love to me. Now."

CHAPTER 7

*S*heryl had never been an overly assertive woman but for the first time in her life she knew with absolute certainty what she wanted, and she wasn't going to back down. She told herself she was doing this to wipe off the memory of Sloan especially since they were supposed to be getting married tomorrow in LA. But she knew the truth even if she tried to deny it to herself. She didn't want Michael in her bed because she wanted to get over Sloan or to prove she had. She wanted him because something about him called to her; he was fun, exciting, annoying, and so handsome she sometimes forgot to breathe just looking at him.

She just wanted… him. Period.

She wasn't going to waste time explaining her decision to herself she decided. But it seemed as though he needed an explanation.

He hadn't closed his mouth since her announcement, and she was starting to feel awkward.

She shifted from one foot to the other, feeling more than a little tacky and awkward. *Maybe I shouldn't have come out naked? Maybe this was too much? Maybe you didn't blindside a guy with this?*

But what was she supposed to have done? She wanted him so much that she was almost going out of her mind, but he had been avoiding her as though she had the plague ever since that one time he had touched her and apologized profusely for it.

She cocked an eyebrow, "Well?"

He swallowed, "Are you sure?"

It sounded more like a croak and so unlike his usual self-assured self and for the first time she relaxed. He wanted her too she realized with a dizzying rush of relief.

She crooked her forefinger like some femme fatale in an old Western, "C'mere"

That was all she got out before he zoomed across the room and plastered her against the wall. His hands were everywhere all at once, exciting and making her moan as she flung her hands around his neck.

He kissed her deeply, his tongue stroking hers in bold sweeping strokes. "I've wanted to do this since I first clapped eyes on you," he whispered against her lips.

His mouth trailed down to her neck even as his hands began to knead the soft skin of her breast. She moaned, letting him kiss her and make love to her with his lips.

Michael let his left hand drift down to the juncture of her thighs and Sheryl spread her legs for him, letting him stroke her where she was damp with desire. He began to dip a hand into her pussy, thrusting it in and out, in and out in slow unhurried motions.

Sheryl gasped feeling passion skyrocket through her as he touched her.

"You're so wet for me," he whispered.

She grabbed his dick through the thick material of his

pants, "You're hard for me too. Hard and hot; my two favorite H factors. I like it."

Her hands made quick work of his fly and she dipped her hand inside, letting a small moan escape her as she found his wet, velvety tip. He was hard as a rock and so huge the thick bulbous head of his dick filled her small palm completely.

She began to move her palm up and down over his hard length, making him groan.

"Think we should take this to the bed?" he groaned.

She threw him a saucy grin, "Too tame. Right here against the wall is what I need," she finished as she turned around and presented her buttocks to him.

He groaned and bent her forward and entered her in one quick stroke even as his other hand slapped against her buttocks. He was so huge and thick he filled her up tight and he wasn't even inside of her to the hilt yet. His hands encircled her slim body, stroking her breasts and holding her in place as he began to ram in and out of her fucking her with an increasingly fast rhythm that made her breasts jiggle.

Sheryl threw back her head, her eyes shut as a kaleidoscope of colors exploded behind her eyes. He dipped one hand down her front and brushed the flat of one hand against her clitoris. She moaned and spread wider for him.

"That's it, baby. You're so fucking tight," he groaned as he slapped her ass and watched it jiggle in response again.

He paused in his thrusts and bent her over completely until she was at a ninety degrees angle. He turned her a little, still joined at the groin, so the wall was on her right. Then he resumed thrusting. Sheryl was almost gasping for breath; caught up in the pleasure of what he was doing to her.

"Michael, that feels so good. Don't stop," she moaned cupping her breasts in her own hands.

He fisted a hand in her hair, pulling her head backwards

and another hand cupped one breast holding her in place as he fucked her harder and harder.

Pleasure roared through her in a blinding rush, and she screamed his name aloud as she came in wave after wave of crashing pleasure. When she was spent, he lifted her into his arms and carried her to the bed. As he placed her onto it and followed her down, her eyes popped open in surprise.

His grin was pure wicked mischief as he assured her in a silky tone that made her nipples twitch in response, "I'm not done with you yet. That wild wall sex was to satisfy your wanton side. But this? This one is for me."

Then with aching tenderness, he bent his head to her breasts and began to suckle her nipples with slow, gentle strokes of his tongue that made every last one of her toes curl.

"I've wanted to do a leisurely exploration of your entire body since I clapped eyes on you. I was fascinated by your thin waist, your soft skin, your beautiful lips," he crooned talking to her in the low tone often reserved for petting babies.

Sheryl could feel her whole body and her entire being responding to his tenderness and his gentleness. She didn't want this, she thought shifting restlessly. She wanted wild fucking that reminded her this was just sex so she wouldn't get too attached. She didn't want aching tenderness and gentle lovemaking that made her feel... things she had no business feeling. She didn't want to see him looking at her with such tenderness in his molten gaze as though she were the only woman on earth. She didn't want to develop feelings for him; feelings were inconvenient, and she would only end up right where she was when Sloan fucked out of her life.

Just then Michael's lips drifted down to her stomach and she stiffened. Sloan had always had something unpleasant to say about the small scar on her stomach left by the fibroid surgery she had undergone. She cursed under her breath because she had been so lost in the moment that she had forgotten and allowed Michael to see it. That was why she had learned to make love with her stomach turned away so she wouldn't irritate Sloan too much.

Anger coursed through her now and she lay stiff as a board waiting for Michael to be repelled by her scar. She was done apologizing because she wasn't pretty as a feather and perfect as the wind.

Sure enough, he paused when he reached the scar and Sheryl sternly assured herself that that wasn't her heart breaking all over again. She didn't care what he thought because he didn't matter; it didn't matter. This was just sex.

Just then his tongue poked out and licked the scar with reverent gentleness. And that's when her control broke. She burst into tears as he licked her scar gently and she felt him rear up in perplexed surprise.

"Does it still hurt?" he asked with urgent concern. "Can I get you something?"

She shook her head, opening her eyes enough to see the confusion and fear in his eyes. He was a good, good, man and she had no right to compare him to *Le Bastard*. In a flash of clarity, she knew that they weren't just having sex; they were making *love*.

She cupped his face with both hands and pulled him down for a searing kiss of her own. She knew he noticed and liked the difference in her touch because he immediately got into it as she poured all of herself into the kiss.

When she let him lift his head, she could *feel* the emotions which were shining from her eyes and she didn't care. She wanted him to see them. She wanted him to feel them. She loved him as she had never loved anyone, she thought.

That realization was staggering, and she frowned. Love? Where had that come from?

As though he had read her thoughts, he cupped her cheek and whispered, "Whatever you feel right now is normal Sheryl. I feel it too. Don't pull away from me. Let's enjoy each other for tonight."

She nodded. He was right. Tomorrow was soon enough to worry about thoughts, feelings and emotions, and what they meant. For tonight, they had each other and that was enough.

She spread her legs wide for him and watched in dazed pleasure as he lowered his head between her legs. His tongue flicked against her soft clitoris and she moaned and spread even wider for him. He began to make love to her pussy with his mouth, kissing, tasting and sucking until she was a quivering mass of sensation and orgasm. He dipped one long finger into her tight wet pussy, stroking in and out as he continued to suck her pussy.

"Please don't make me cum again so soon," Sheryl pleaded pushing at his shoulders. "I want you to cum instead."

He didn't answer. He just kept right on licking and kissing and stroking until she came in a hot, pulsating shower of indecent, decadent pleasure. Her thighs shook, her belly quivered, her entire being shattered. And when she was done, he kissed her softly and praised her for being such a 'good girl' then he spread her legs and shoved into her once more.

As he began to make love to her, Sheryl moaned and groaned, spreading her legs wider and letting him love her. Her hands clutched his forearms which were on either side of her to support his weight and her legs were spread as wide as they would go.

He looked up at her then, gauging her reaction and something moved in his eyes; something dark, wild, animal, and frightening. Then he blinked and smiled, and it was gone; the harsh planes and angles of his face were once more replaced with the smiling face of her lover.

He kissed her reassuringly on the cheek, then he trailed his lips to her mouth and began to kiss her. The kisses were light at first, but then the kiss deepened, and she forgot everything else and wound her arms around him. He was a master at caressing her and transporting her to heights she had never even suspected existed.

His fat penis glided in and out of her and she moaned with each thrust, her hands and legs gliding over his skin as she urged him on with ragged cries while undulating her hips in a helpless reaction.

She reached a hand between and cupped his balls in a gentle caress as he thrust in and out in repeated, dizzyingly delightful motions. The unexpected caress on his balls seemed to throw him off course and he gasped and let out a moan, his head falling backward as he released a guttural sound from the back of his throat.

"You witch!" he groaned. Then he rested his forehead against hers and began to move again, pumping his hips for all he was worth.

Waves of ecstasy enveloped them, and their cries of pleasure mingled as they both drank their fill of each other. Michael increased the tempo of his thrusts, riding her hard as he gathered her even more tightly in his arms. The shift in position heightened Sheryl's awareness and the resultant sensation and before she knew what to expect, she was pulsing, clenching and unclenching around him as her body found release yet again. The force of her fulfillment shook Michael to his very core, and he threw back his head, grunting as he thrust one last time into her before spilling his seed deep into her in rapid successive spurts.

When he was spent, they both drifted slowly back to earth and Sheryl let him see the incredulity in her eyes.

"That was…" she began, drifting into silence as words failed her.

He chuckled as he bent forward and rubbed his nose against hers. "Yes, it was."

He kissed her softly, then withdrew. "I need to use the bathroom. I imagine you do too."

She laughed and nodded.

As soon as the door closed behind him, something began to vibrate on the floor. She lifted herself with a frown as she regarded the jeans on the floor. What could be vibrating? She had watched him destroy his only phone.

With a frown, she got out of bed and padded toward the jeans on the floor. A small cellphone fell into her hand and she stared at it. He had lied when he said he had destroyed the phone.

No, she had seen the pieces. This was a spare phone then. Anger and betrayal swept through her. She started to toss the phone aside when the call hung up and a text message flashed across the screen from someone named Hannah:

Where are you, Michael? Your brothers won't say, and I'm getting worried. Hurry home this instant. Love ya.

Sheryl felt the world tilt on its axis. Who was Hannah? Had she just helped Michael cheat on his wife or girlfriend?

CHAPTER 8

Something was eating Sheryl up, but she wouldn't say what, Michael thought flicking her a glance for the umpteenth time. He was making good on his promise to take her back to town this morning. He had already begun packing up their few belongings and taking them out to show he meant business, but she hadn't even managed to dredge up more than a wan smile. What was bothering her?

Did she perhaps regret their lovemaking? He tried to pretend it wouldn't matter if she regretted it, but he couldn't. He had enjoyed making love to her so much and she had enjoyed it too as far as he knew; heck she had reached orgasm three times but who was counting?

He felt a grunt, or was it a growl, again. It carried a mixture of desire, pride and possession all wrapped up in a primal mix.

Of course I want her to be satisfied, he though, *to feel good.*

He didn't want to admit to himself how the thought of her unhappiness was making him feel. *Ungrounded. That was the word...*

She had worn the clothes he had given her this morning

and seeing her in them, he had almost regretted his actions. The bum-shorts emphasized the curve of her hips and the top lay sleek and smooth over her body. She was devastatingly beautiful. Her short curls lay in layers around her face and her feminine scent rose to assail his nostrils, stirring his Wolf and igniting raw, unbridled hunger inside of him.

With great effort, he forced down the need swirling inside of him and focused on her face. It was aloof and unwelcoming.

"Everything okay?" he asked as he buttered some more bread for her.

She took the proffered slice woodenly which was pretty much the way she had reacted to everything else since their lovemaking. He sighed now, recalling how he had come out of the bathroom already joking about taking a shower together when she had levered off the bed, thanked him for 'showing her a nice time' with a politeness that made him want to throw something, and then she had shut the bathroom door in his face once more. When she had emerged, it had been obvious she had taken the time to scrub off the evidence of his lovemaking and this time she hadn't even balked at using cold water.

Did she find his touch repulsive then? But she had seemed to like it just fine when he had been making love to her, he thought in frustration. Was this a bad case of buyers' remorse then?

Her profile was as serene as a lake and blank as a doll, he saw as he flicked her an annoyed glance. Her very calmness while he was going through such inner turmoil pissed him off. He wanted to give her a rough hard shake if that would jar her out of her hunky-dory existence. But somehow, he feared that even that wouldn't affect her one bit or dredge up much of a response beyond a couple of boring placating words; she was as distant and unresponsive as the moon!

"Sheryl. I don't play games because I don't understand them, and I don't like them. If there is something you're trying to say to me, get it out here in the open so we can deal with it. I don't like this silent treatment; it's driving me crazy."

She lifted her gaze to his then and that was when he saw it: a well of hurt was in her brown eyes. She looked very hurt. Her eyes were dulled with sadness and everything in him tightened in automatic rejection of the notion that he had put that look in her eyes.

As she held his gaze, a sheen of tears shimmered in her eyes, but she blinked them away and faced away from him again, as silent as a tomb.

He swallowed, falling silent in the face of that incontrovertible evidence that she regretted everything that had transpired between them.

His voice almost broke as he reached for her hand, "Tell me please. What's wrong?"

She looked down at his hand on her arm, apparently willing him to remove it. He left it there in stubbornness.

She looked back up at him, "I found your *other* cellphone."

He nodded, encouraging her to continue.

She sighed, as though drawing on a reserve of strength she didn't know she had as she continued, while watching him out of shuttered eyes. "Hannah sent you a message. She wanted you to hurry home."

He frowned trying to follow what could possibly be upsetting about that. So, he hadn't come out right and admitted that he had another phone but that didn't mean she had to be upset. Of course, she could understand that he had been willing to do just about anything to keep her safe and he had been worried a phone call to whatever family she had might have been intercepted or traced by Roy.

"Listen, Roy knows who you are, so chances are, he's

watching your family. I was just being careful," he protested. "That's why I didn't tell you about the phone."

She stared at him in fascination as though he were from another planet then she shook her head in that way women did that made them all the more mysterious to the male of the specie. "You don't get it, do you?" she charged.

He shook his own head. "No."

With a hiss, she pushed away from the table and stalked toward the door, "Let's just get out of here."

He sighed. Talk about crash and burn. But he couldn't very well let her walk out of here without trying and explaining what sort of danger she was in; at least he could tell her about the vampires. He wasn't sure she was ready to hear about his secret yet; she might flip. But his guts said he could trust her.

In all his years he had never felt the urge to trust anyone who wasn't a shifter with information about his abilities and he was all the more confused as to why he should feel that way about someone who wasn't a shifter.

But something about Sheryl calmed him and made him feel… well, safe with her. It was a strange development to him, he thought. He was the one who was used to calming people down using his gifts. He was the most strategic and the most brilliant of all the Exotic Pack, so he was used to being the one to come up with ideas and game plans and the one to try to make everyone feel safe. He had never really thought about how *he* felt until Sheryl came into his life.

She was something else all right. Whatever he had done with her, it hadn't been just sex. It had run soul deep which was why his entire being rejected any notion of regret on her part.

"Wait. There's something you should know," he called. "It's not gonna be easy to say it, and you may not believe me, but you have to hear this."

Something indefinable passed across her features, then she muttered with disgust, "I already know what you're going to say. You made me the other woman, didn't you? God, I feel like I'm gonna be sick!"

The other woman? What the hell did she mean by that, he wondered. She didn't give him a chance to say anything else though. She wrenched open the front door and froze. A man was perched on the other side of the door frame.

Michael's nostrils picked up the sickly-sweet scent that spelled vampire even before the newcomer said a word. In a flash Michael was at the door, shoving Sheryl back inside and planting himself in the doorway instead, his large frame preventing the vampire from gaining entry.

The vampire grinned like the proverbial Cheshire cat as he sang, "Yep. I knew I was gonna be the one to find her. Then when the king hears it, I'm gonna be the first one he rewards with the Sunlight Ring."

Great, just great, Michael thought, while filing away the information that the sort of ring Roy used had a name: Sunlight Ring. This vampire, though, didn't have a ring on, so how was he out in daylight?

"Get away from her," Michael barked. "Besides, your kind has to be invited in, right? I'm not doing any inviting."

"Oh, don't be such a… beast. I'm sure the little lady wants to play with me," the vampire laughed.

Michael peered at the sun which was still in the sky, "How are you able to walk in daylight?"

The vampire shrugged, "Roy made me a tiny vial; probably something made with his ring's contents. It's temporary, but it's good enough to allow me to move around to find her. C'mere sweetie," he cooed.

"Fuck off," Michael spat.

"Why are you chasing him away, Michael?" Sheryl demanded. "He seems to have been searching for me. Maybe

Kate sent out a search party," she said striding forward. Her shin brushed against the jagged edge of the center table as she came, and she gasped as a thin line of blood welled from the small cut and began a red liquid trail down her leg.

As though in slow motion, Michael swiveled his head to look at the vampire, gauging the unavoidable effect on the man. As soon as the man caught the whiff of blood from Sheryl's injury, his eyes turned red, and his fangs shot out immediately in rapacious hunger as he made to dive past Michael.

Sheryl saw his fangs appear and she screamed. The sound galvanized Michael into action. Without stopping to think about it, he leaped onto the vampire and rolled with him in the dirt, leaves and dirt flying everywhere, as they began to swing blows. The vampire was in his element, using his supernatural strength while Michael was disadvantaged fighting in human form. He saw Sheryl watching with rounded eyes and he knew she was already scared enough. If he changed into his shifter form just then she might not be able to bear it.

The vampire bared his fangs to bite Michael and with a muffled oath, Michael jerked away in time. As he rolled, he saw the vampire leap toward the cabin to get at Sheryl. With a loud howl, Michael changed into his Wolf form. He heard Sheryl give a bloodcurdling scream this time, the sound almost hysterical, and he dimly realized she must be in shock.

He ignored her and threw himself once more into the fight. He howled as he bent his head and bit into the vampire's leg. The vampire hit him across the face, trying to shake him off. He bit down harder.

With a sob, the vampire jerked his foot from the Wolf's mouth and limped a few feet away, his hands raised in the classic sign of surrender.

Michael growled low in his throat, his fur bristling as he only just held back himself from attacking the vampire again.

"You got it, man. You got it. This is your turf," the vampire called. "I'm backing off."

Michael debated the wisdom of letting the vampire go. The man would only run off to warn Roy. His mind made up, he leaped on the vampire again, crashing the vampire to the ground even as the vampire howled in pain and began to struggle in earnest. Using his abilities, he forced the man to calm down, his Wolf's gaze still locked on the man's.

Once the vampire had quieted and was fully under his influence, Michael locked gaze with him, growling low in his throat as he began to compel the vampire into forgetting all about being here. When Michael was done, the vampire passed out and was frighteningly still. He knew the effect of the compulsion he had exercised on the vampire would not wear off for at least a couple of hours which meant the vampire would be unconscious for a long time.

Slowly Michael turned around to face Sheryl. She was frozen in the doorway, her face as white as a sheet as she stared transfixed at his Wolf form. With an inward sigh, he changed back into his human form and stood tall in front of her.

He took one step forward, "Sheryl."

With a small cry, she retreated into the house and slammed the door shut in his face. "Stay away from me! Stay the hell away from me."

Fantastic, he thought with a weary sigh. He never seemed to get any breaks, he thought as he wiped one hand down his face.

He turned and grabbed the vampire by the shirt collar lifted him onto his shoulder and took him to the edge of a sloping hill. He gave the man a small kick with his leg and the prone vampire began to roll down the hill. He watched until the man was at the bottom of the hill and he nodded with satisfaction.

By the time the vampire woke up, he wouldn't remember anything about being in the cabin and he would simply wander away and return home. Besides, by then, he would be long gone with Sheryl, Michael thought. Of course, that depended on whether she let him anywhere near her.

He knocked on the cabin door. "Sheryl? I'm coming in. I don't want to alarm you, but we need to talk."

Silence.

He knocked again.

Just then he heard the unmistakable whirr of his motorbike's engine at the back of the cabin. He raced out and found Sheryl behind the wheel, her hands as white as her face as the motor roared to life.

"I won't let you leave without talking to me," he told her.

"You're not even human. What's there to talk about?" Sheryl cried.

She was shaking like a leaf but there was an almost desperate glint of determination in her eyes that told him she was bent on escaping him one way or the other.

Damn it. How did one handle this sort of situation, he wondered. How had Theodore handled telling his wife, Jessica, that he wasn't human, he thought thinking of the leader of their Exotic Pack and his human wife who positively adored him and didn't turn so much as a hair when he shifted form around her.

He growled, "I need to talk to you Sheryl. I can explain all this if you will just let me. But don't drive off without me. Come on, you're in danger. You know it's true. You saw that vampire and he wanted a taste of you."

Her eyes were round as she whispered, "All I know is whatever else he may be, at least *he* doesn't turn into a beast. He looks human enough to me. What are you?"

His Wolf side growled inside of him at the reference to a beast. He was anything but. He was controlled, organized and more human than most humans. Plus, he was nothing like that vampire. The man would have torn her limb from limb if Michael hadn't intervened. Couldn't she decipher that?

"Go on," Sheryl prodded, still so frightened she was almost hysterical. "What other animal can you turn into? Why didn't you tell me you were a beast?"

He countered swiftly, "I'm a shifter not a beast."

He had yelled the words in his frustration, and she quieted at once, staring at him as though she were seeing him for the first time. Something in her eyes shifted and he knew with absolute certainty that at last they were past the hysterical stage her shock had shoved her into. And not a moment too soon. He wasn't sure he could handle hearing her call him a beast again. It hurt too much when she said it. If it were anyone else, it would roll off him like stone on water; he had been called worse after all. But this was Sheryl and what she thought of him mattered a lot whether he wanted it to or not.

She was still staring at him in wide-eyed silence, as though she wasn't quite certain what to make of him.

"Please just get off the bike and we can discuss this like two calm rational adults. I swear I won't hurt you. Come on it's me. You know I would never hurt you," he told her. The words were said very calmly but deep down he felt as though this was a *Kairos* moment in his dealings with her. If she could trust him even a smidgen right now, it would make a world of difference.

Sheryl set her face in the stubborn lines he was fast becoming familiar with as she turned off the motorbike and responded, "Except I've been hurting ever since I met you Michael, haven't I? And even when I tried to leave, you wouldn't let me leave. You were that Wolf in the forest, weren't you?"

The words, unexpected and hitting so close to home, pierced his heart like an arrow and he stumbled backwards subconsciously as though to distance himself from the pain.

"What?" he whispered, the sound almost inaudible.

She got off the motorbike, flinging her hands as she ticked off his offences. "First you whisked me away and cut me off from Kate who by the way is hypertensive and must be beside herself with worry now. Then you wouldn't tell me why I was sequestered away with a strange man in a cabin in the woods except that you had the unmitigated gall to assure me that the kidnapping was 'for my own good.' Next you were intimate with me but somehow in between that you forgot to mention that there was a certain Hannah waiting for you somewhere who loves you and wants you to hurry home. Then the big one: you're not even human! *How* could you keep such a big secret from me? Correction: secrets?"

"Sheryl, I don't know what you're referring to but of course Hannah wants me to come home; she's my oldest friend in the whole world so why wouldn't she? Next, we only met three days ago. Was I supposed to spill my entire secrets to a virtual stranger?"

"We were already intimate. I would hardly call it being strangers!" she yelled. "Didn't I deserve the simple respect of making my own choice on whether I wanted to be intimate with another specie of creation *before* the act?"

When she put it that way, he saw her point, he thought. He wasn't human and she had the right to her reservations. Maybe she thought he wasn't good enough for her being a shifter and all.

The thought burned like acid in the back of his throat and his voice was a bit harder than he had intended as he growled, "I wanted you so bad Sheryl and I'm not gonna apologize for that. One glance at you naked, and I knew I had to have you. I could hardly have stopped right in the middle of foreplay to say, 'Hey, guess what? I'm a shifter in my spare time.' That wouldn't have gone over so well I'm thinking," he growled pushed past all endurance by what he saw as an unfair attack.

Maybe she had a right to be angry and all, but the one thing he just could not bear was any insinuation that he had taken advantage of her because they had both been right there; she had wanted him every bit as much as he had wanted her, and he was damned if he was going to let her get away with pretending otherwise even for a minute. Hell, she had even put the moves on him with that naked act; not that he was complaining. He thought she had never looked more glorious and beautiful, and he knew even if he never saw her again, he would take that memory to his grave.

He wasn't going to let her pretend or insinuate that she regretted their lovemaking, he thought with such fervor that his Wolf stirred in agreement. His Wolf quivered with possessiveness and an insistence that signaled its desire to mate with her again and again. She was his and damned if he would let her backpedal on him.

And he absolutely refused to examine why it mattered so very much to him that she didn't regret their lovemaking. It mattered and that was that.

Sheryl looked shocked for a minute, and then to his utter surprise and stupefied delight, she burst into great gales of laughter.

Now he was confused, Michael thought as he stared at her in absolute wonder. But even now, watching her laugh at who knew what, he couldn't squelch the feeling of possessive pride that swelled in him.

She was gorgeous, she was delightful, she was absolutely breathtaking. She was *his*.

His Wolf stirred in agreement. She was his mate, he thought with more force, and in that moment, he knew he had never been more certain of anything else in his life.

She was *his!* She was his mate for life, and it didn't matter that he hadn't marked her. She was in his blood and he was in hers.

CHAPTER 9

*S*heryl's laughter began to die down as she saw the unmistakable possessive gleam kindle in his eyes. The molten lava burned brighter and hotter as he looked at her burning like smoldering coals with a heat that seemed as though it could have scalded her. Her laughter faded underneath the intense fire burning in his eyes as an answering flame flickered and came to life inside of her.

She knew that look. She recognized it at a deep primal level, and she felt an answering awareness kick in the pits of her stomach as her entire being reacted to him. She wasn't afraid of him, despite knowing he could turn into a Wolf, she realized. She couldn't deny that she was curious and, in a way, excited by the inherent danger in entangling with a shifter. She had been scared at first of course, but she knew he would never harm her. Knowing he could turn into a Wolf at will was strange to say the least; she had never even imagined such a possibility. Sure, she had read books and seen movies, but she had really just thought that was all fiction. Now she could hardly deny the evidence of her own eyes; she had seen him morph into a Wolf and then back into human form with as much fuss as one changing a shirt.

His gaze was still locked on hers as he started to walk toward her, his eyes still smoldering with that secret fire she had always wondered about. She realized now that the strange color of his eyes contrasted beautifully with his white fur when he was in Wolf form.

His golden eyes are a dead giveaway of the powerful Wolf locked away inside of him; it's a wonder I didn't sense it sooner, she thought. *But then, how could I have? Up until a few minutes ago, I wouldn't have believed it was possible for a human being to morph into anything else. I've always chalked it up to Sci-Fi.* Michael was still staring at her with that burning intensity he did so well. His gaze was doing strange things to her insides; her nipples were hardening into fine points and she couldn't deny the pool of wetness gathering in her pussy.

"Don't look at me that way," she said, almost pleading, as she took a few steps backwards for self-preservation.

He quirked an eyebrow, "Is there a particular way I'm looking at you?"

She nodded. "Like I'm an ice cream cone on a sunny day."

He chuckled, stepping closer, "You do feel like an ice cream cone on a sunny day to me."

She let herself stare into his eyes, drinking in his absolute magnetism and luxuriating in that indescribable joy that welled up deep inside of her when she was this close to him.

"Why were you laughing just now?" he asked.

She shrugged, "Well, you said something about being a shifter in your spare time and it made me laugh."

He reached out and stroked a gentle hand down one of her cheeks. "I want you to always laugh and be happy Sheryl. I swear I didn't lie to you on purpose but it's a delicate truth and I couldn't just blurt it out. I *was* going to tell you, right before the vampire showed up at the door."

Her eyes darkened with unhappy memory. "Was he one of the guys after me?"

Michael looked at her as though weighing what to tell her. She took his hand from her cheek and turned it palm up before placing a small kiss in the middle of that hand. "You can tell me the truth Michael. Don't try to shield me."

"There aren't a few 'guys' after you Sheryl. There are hordes of vampires after you. I saw them pass your scent around with your scrunchy."

She paled a little, trying to wrap her mind around that. So that was how her favorite scrunchy had gotten missing. She dimly remembered a scene from *Twilight* where the vampires had decided the heroine had to die and had passed her scent around so any vampire anywhere could pick her out of a crowd and ... well, drink her to death. That hadn't been fun. And she was learning now that that hadn't been just fiction either.

She peeked up at him from beneath her long lashes, brown eyes clouded with confusion. "So, what does that mean? Every vampire on earth suddenly has it in for me?"

He shrugged, "Maybe just those who acknowledge Roy as king."

She stared off into the distance, her heart thumping. That didn't sound much better. This Roy person, whomever he was, seemed to have some clout in the vampire world. If she was in danger, then it might be best if she stayed away from Kate for now. She didn't want to be a compass that pointed maniacal vengeful vampires in the direction of her only sister and her little kid.

"How serious are we talking and how long before this blows over?" she asked.

He met her gaze with sincerity shining in the depths of his eyes. "I'm not gonna lie to you, it's serious. Kinda like being on the Mafia's hit list. Think of a *most wanted* list."

Okay, that sounded serious, she thought. With a sigh she dropped his hand and headed back to the cabin.

"What are you doing now?" he called after her.

Sheryl paused and turned to face him, "Well, if I'm on some sort of list, I've decided I won't go out without a fight. Come on in and teach me all you can about these creatures. I'm gonna kick their ass before I let them get me."

His smile was like that of a proud papa. "I knew you were pure dynamite but honey you've exceeded even my own expectations. Come on Buffy, let's get your training wheels on," he chortled flinging an arm around her and drawing her to his side as they headed toward the cabin.

As soon as they were in, he led her to the cushion and settled in, pulling her down beside him. He dragged over a small coffee table, his gaze locked on hers. "What do you want to know?"

"First tell me about yourself. How did you get to be a shifter?" she asked.

He shrugged, "I was born this way. I mean I wasn't always a shifter per se, but as soon as I was about nine or ten years old, my body started changing. Both my parents were shifters you know. It happens that way with shifter kids generally."

Sheryl saw the faint hint of sadness darkening his eyes as he spoke of his parents and her heart turned over in her chest as she covered his hand with hers, "Were?"

He nodded, "They were killed. Roy Davison is an old enemy. His father was Atlas Corning, a vicious old vampire. Atlas convinced the townspeople that my folks were the vampires killing people around town. I think he may have compelled them a little too. They lost their humanity, went drunk with a need for vengeance and absolutely berserk with bloodlust. They burned my folks at the stake along with the parents of all the others."

The story was too surreal and vivid, and yet he recounted it in a cool voice, devoid of emotion. He seemed more than a little detached. She grabbed both his hands, "You were a little boy when all of this happened. How did you survive?"

He shrugged, "I had the Pack; they became my brothers. We had each other."

"The Pack?"

"The Exotic Pack. Six shifters bound by cords of love, loyalty and a lifetime together. Theodore is our leader. He's a bear. Connor's a dragon—"

"Wait. Back up. A real life, honest to goodness dragon?" she demanded her eyes shining like stars in her excitement.

Her openness and seeming naiveté made him laugh. "Yes Sheryl. He's a real life, honest to goodness dragon."

"Oh my God. Let's leave right now. I want to meet him," she screamed in excitement as she made to hurtle from the chair.

He laughed as he pulled her back down, "Simmer down. He's probably still on honeymoon with his new pregnant wife so I doubt he's signing autographs at the moment."

Sheryl's eyes narrowed. Had he gone out of his way to inform her that Connor was married and therefore unavailable? Or was it her imagination? She liked the idea of him being jealous, she thought her eyes shining as she decided to tease him some more. Besides, she wanted to know for sure if he were jealous; that would be so sweet. She also thought of him in a possessive light which was why she flown off the handle when she had seen Hannah's message and imagined the worst. Sure, she still had some trust issues and baggage left over from her relationship with *Le Bastard* but even if she didn't, she was a normal red-blooded woman which meant she didn't like to share, thank you very much.

She wrinkled her nose at Michael, "Is he big, bad and strong?"

He gave her an irritated glare, "He isn't bigger than me by much. Just an inch or half an inch really. He has really big ears and teeth anyway," he added with something approaching the sort of petulant pout she sometimes saw on the faces of her kids back at school.

Sheryl swallowed a shout of laughter and appeased him with a gentle murmur "He sounds thoroughly boring for a dragon. What about your other brothers?"

He brightened at once as he began to tell her about Darryl the deer shifter who could read minds, Jonathan the Panther shifter who was the most mischievous and fun loving of the group and Justin the lion shifter who was the most laidback and self-effacing of the group.

"And the vampires. How do we defeat them? Salt? Silver? Stake?" she asked as their conversation came full circle.

He frowned, apparently taken aback, "Salt? Sheryl what sort of movies have you been watching? They're vampires not earthworms."

She couldn't help it, she dissolved into laughter bending over as she released great whoops of mirth.

He laughed with her, the sound warm and deep and flowing over her like warm chocolate.

Sheryl's eyes met his and the laughter died in her throat. "Well, considering they're trying so very hard to kill me, you can't blame me for likening them to creepy crawlies like worms. I hate worms."

He gave her a boyish grin, "All girls hate worms."

He reached out one hand and pushed her hair gently off her face. She moaned and turned her head a little to the side to plant a kiss on his palm.

His breath hissed out in reaction and he delved his hand into her hair and pulled her face closer to his. Their mouths met in a wild swooping kiss. His other hand encircled her waist, guiding her body frame onto his until she was sitting astride his lap and they were entangled in a passionate embrace.

"How does it feel being with a human? Being with me? Isn't it kind of weird?" she asked, pausing to look into his eyes.

"It doesn't feel the least bit weird. It's the most wonderful feeling in the entire world. Making love with you completes me and makes me feel like the luckiest man alive."

Sheryl felt the truth of that sink into the deepest parts of her being and she managed to keep from blushing.

I like what I'm hearing, she thought. *He makes me feel like the sexiest woman alive when he looks at me with such hot longing in his eyes.*

His hands hungrily kneaded her breasts, squeezing the soft flesh almost painfully through the light material of her top. She gasped in reaction and thrust her chest forward, eager for more of his touch. Brimming with impatience, he shoved the tank top and her bra upwards in one fluid motion and bent his head to take one thrusting nipple in his mouth.

Sheryl moaned and held him even closer, enjoying the raw passion unleashed inside of him as though he couldn't get enough of her. He sucked her hard, drawing the nipple into his mouth again and again and flicking the sensitive tip with his tongue. Sheryl wriggled in his arms, wanting even more and unable to marshal her thoughts enough to form words of encouragement.

He didn't seem to need words though. He lowered her to the floor and unzipped her shorts. He lowered them to her knees and all the way past her ankles. He spread her legs and returned his lips to her breast. His hand stroked her open thighs, before pushing her panties to the side and dipping into her pussy.

"You're so fucking wet," he murmured against her breast.

Sheryl shifted, restless and eager to feel his touch inside

of her. "Go inside Michael. Go deep. Do it now."

He chuckled, "Your impatience is hot."

He stroked his finger in gentle motions against the soft sensitive skin of her clitoris and then he began to move the very tip of his forefinger in round little circles over the nub of her clitoris, his touch so light it was barely there. His mouth was still feasting on her breasts.

The pleasure shot straight to her brain and she screamed, spreading her legs even wider, "Oh yes. Yes. How did you know? Just there! Yes."

He continued the tender stroking of her clitoris, his finger forming small circles on the tiny sensitive flesh in repeated motions that made her pussy begin to clench in reaction. Sheryl grabbed his shoulder, buffeted on a wave of passion as she grunted and moaned in his arms. Vaginal juices flooded her pussy making her entrance wet and slippery as he dipped one finger into her vagina. She groaned and began to move her hips up and down as he began to thrust into her pussy again and again. Passion rose, exploding behind her eyes like a kaleidoscope of colors. Her nails dug into his back as she shuddered convulsively beneath him.

He paused and flipped her onto her stomach on the floor, lifted her to her knees and spread her legs even wider as he positioned his dick at her entrance and took her from behind. His first thrust shoved him inside her to the hilt, the intensity telling her that he was as turned on as she was.

Sheryl twisted her waist, enjoying herself as he began to pound away at her pussy in earnest, increasing the tempo of his thrusts even as she arched her back, pressing her buttocks hard against his thrusting pelvis. Waves of ecstasy enveloped Sheryl and her cries of pleasure increased with the tempo of his thrusts.

Tension coiled in her belly like a spring, her stomach

clenched harder and harder until she was screaming loudly. He flipped her onto her back again and bent down and began sucking her breasts using his teeth and tongue until she was moaning and groaning.

Michael slid into her again in slow sure thrusts as though savoring her tightness as she clamped down around him with her tight vaginal walls. He slapped her ass as he entered her to the hilt, startling a moan of mingled surprise, pain and pleasure from her throat. He slapped her ass again and began to thrust into her.

"Oh my! I love that," Sheryl moaned beneath him as he filled her tightly.

"Yes! I love that you are so wet for me," he moaned as he increased the tempo of his thrusts, sliding in and out of her faster and faster and faster.

Sheryl's hands fisted on his forearms, clinging on for dear life as Michael pounded away at her pussy, going so deep she could have sworn he touched her womb. She undulated beneath him, twisting her hips in circles as pleasure racked her entire body.

Soon, Sheryl was pulsing, clenching and unclenching around him as her body found release yet again. Michael leaned down and kissed her, swallowing her cries of pleasure as an orgasm shook her entire frame.

The force of her fulfillment seemed to shake Michael because he was grunting incoherently as he threw back his head in the throes of passion. He thrust one last time into her before spilling his seed deep into her in rapid successive spurts.

Silence reigned as they both collapsed onto the floor, unable to move so much as a limb.

As she floated back to earth, a thought occurred, and Sheryl's eyes widened in consternation even as she sat up in shock. Her tone was distressed as she voiced what she had just realized, "You didn't use a condom! Today and even the last time."

His eyes met hers but before he could respond they heard the unmistakable sound of a car door thudding closed.

Michael leaped to his feet, alert at once, as he yanked his pants back into place. Sheryl scrambled to adjust her top and bra and dashed into the bathroom with her panties and shorts dangling from her hands. She was still tugging on her panties in the bathroom when she heard the cabin door fly open, as though blown off its hinges by the force of a blow.

It wasn't the vampires was it? Please Lord let it not be vampires, she thought feverishly as she pulled on her shorts and began to do up the zipper.

As she reached for the doorknob, she heard squeals of excitement and a loud booming voice announce, "Well, well, well. We were worried sick about you because we thought you were dead in a ditch somewhere and here you are, all holed up, cozy and safe in your getaway."

Sheryl drew open the bathroom door in time to see a short petite woman fling herself into Michael's arms and pepper his face all over with kisses, laughing as she announced, "You're crazy, you know that? I thought you were dead for sure. You had me so worried."

"Hannah," Michael breathed as he buried his face in her neck and hugged her back tightly as though he would never let go.

The blood drained from Sheryl's face as she watched their closeness. This was *the* Hannah Walker then.

She looked around at the gathered crowd of five men and three women and surmised that this had to be his family. From the way he had described them, she could tell his five shifter brothers were the men in the room and the other two women had to be Julia and Jessica. Her eyes were drawn unerringly though to the third woman Hannah; she had yet to disentangle herself from Michael's arms and even Sheryl had to admit that she looked like she belonged there. What had Michael called her? A childhood friend who knew all there was to know about him? Sheryl was willing to bet that Hannah also knew he was a shifter too and didn't have a problem with that.

She wasn't sure why but seeing him with these people made her feel like an outsider; made her feel like just running away and being by herself. She was just some New Yorker who hadn't known up until a few hours ago that shifters even existed. These people had been together all their lives.

She studied Hannah dropping one more peck onto Michael's cheek again and she sighed within. Maybe Michael hadn't actively lied when he said Hannah was just a friend, but she could see, clear as the nose on her face, that Hannah wanted to be a whole lot more than just a friend. Perhaps she *was* a whole lot more.

Just then, Michael howled with laughter as he picked the small woman up in his arms and turned her around in a circle, all the while laughing like some horny hyena.

Sheryl bit her lip as she regarded the laughing couple, and something struck her at once; something that had bothered her from the moment she saw them together which she had been trying to put her finger on— that hug didn't scream friendship; these two had been intimate. She would stake her life on that.

Just then one of the other men spotted her and boomed, "And who is your friend Michael?"

All eyes turned to focus on her face including Hannah's. Now Sheryl was no mind-reader, but she could read basic moods and expressions. Hannah didn't look too pleased to find another woman sequestered in a tiny cabin alone in the jungle with Michael Bennet. For that matter, neither did any other members of his family.

CHAPTER 10

Michael couldn't believe his good luck that his entire family had descended on the cabin as though this were some planned family vacation and Connor and Theodore had even brought along their wives! Of course, Jessica and Theodore hadn't come with their three kids nor had Darryl come with his two, but it felt like the whole damn family was here just the same.

He had been so eager to introduce Sheryl to every one of them and now, without warning, like a genie granting his wishes, there they were!

When Theodore had demanded to know who his friend was, and everyone's attention turned to Sheryl at once, he had felt his heart skip yet another beat as he caught sight of her standing by the bathroom door looking delightfully disheveled and so beautiful that it made one's heart ache to look at her.

One look at her kiss swollen lips and even a near-sighted man could tell what they had been doing but he was glad none of his family members were rude or had such bad taste as to say something embarrassing.

She is very beautiful, he thought, feeling his heart thud in his chest. *She is fresh and unspoiled; she has no artifice or feminine wiles. She's just wholesome and utterly amazing.*

It was all he could do not to sweep across the room and entangle her in a bold kiss right there in front of everyone.

I've never felt the need to be that expressive of my feelings before, not even when I was with Hannah. But with Sheryl, I feel like staking my claim and shouting it from the rooftop for the whole damn world to hear.

"That's Sheryl Quinn, everyone," he told them. He walked up to her and drew her hand, drawing her into the circle of his family as he announced, "Sheryl? Meet my family. That's Theodore and his wife Jessica, that's Connor and his new wife Julia, that's Darryl, Justin, Jonathan and Hannah."

She gave him an unreadable smile that didn't quite reach her eyes before turning a much warmer one on Connor that made Michael grit his teeth.

"I've always wanted to meet a real-life dragon," Sheryl purred in a tone that made Michael's brows lift in ire. "You guys were my superheroes when I was a kid."

Connor's eyes gleamed as he took her hand in his and bent over it with all the finesse of a French gentleman. "The pleasure is all mine, Sheryl. I see why Michael wanted to keep you all to himself rather than bringing you to Exotic Rescue and introducing you right away to the gang."

He flicked Michael a speaking glance and Michael gritted his teeth harder. Trust Connor to uncover his insecurities about Sheryl's fascination with dragons and trust the other man to tease him about it covertly.

Michael grabbed Sheryl's other hand uncaring of subtleties, and dragged her back to his side, "Sheryl needs to get some rest in here. We can all go outside and let her rest."

Silence fell at that request and he could almost hear the questions in the minds of his family. They had burning questions, he was certain. Apart from Hannah, he had never had another woman in his life and after their relationship had ended three years ago, he had been more than happy to remain single. And they had all teased him without mercy about his decision to remain single in every sense of the word; not even once considering playing the field or starting up another relationship.

Sheryl's chin jutted out stubbornly as she announced with gritty determination, "I'm not a wilting flower. I can hold my own just fine with your family Michael. You don't have to consign me to the cabin like some little woman afraid to face the world, you know."

Whew. It didn't get any blunter than that, he thought not bothering to hide the admiration he knew had kindled in his eyes. He was almost desperate with his longing for her to like his family, to get to know them, but he hadn't expected her to take the initiative. The more he knew about Sheryl, the more he liked her. Even his Wolf approved of her and was a fierce fan.

Theodore's wife, Jessica, gave Sheryl an approving glance, "Ignore him. Come seat by me Sheryl and tell me all about yourself."

Within seconds his entire family was hanging on her every word, roaring with laughter as she narrated how he had kidnapped her when he caught her spying on the same group of vampires he had been spying on.

His heart turned over in his chest when he saw how she dodged Jonathan's verbal landmines with finesse and grace, how she teased Justin out of his quietness, and how she got Connor to stop frowning enough to tell a few jokes. She was getting along so well with his entire family, he noticed with a pleased grin.

He had been standing alone in a corner observing Sheryl and the rest and he was so absorbed in staring at her pretty, vivid features and hanging onto her every word that he didn't even notice when Darryl sidled up to him.

"You've got it bad man. Think you're gonna be able to get her and Hannah to avoid that catfight I sense coming on though?" Darryl demanded.

Michael looked at him with a confused frown. "What catfight? What are you going on about now?"

Darryl rolled his eyes, "Come on even without my mind reading abilities I can sense the tension and hostility between the two women in your life."

Michael protested, "Hannah isn't in my life anymore; at least not that way."

"Tell that to Sheryl. She's been looking daggers at poor Hannah ever since she clapped eyes on her. And to her credit, Hannah's been returning the favor, no holds barred."

Michael flicked his gaze from where Hannah was busy scrolling through her phone sitting slightly apart from the group, to where Sheryl was holding court apparently heedless of the only other uninterested participant in her conversation with the rest.

He shook his head, feeling annoyance at Darryl's persistent interference, "Come on man. Sheryl's the sweetest woman you ever met. She has no quarrel with Hannah."

Darryl laughed and gave him a rough hard clap on his shoulder that would have sent him to his knees had he been a lesser man. "Gawd to be so clueless. Keep it up Mikey."

With his customary whistle, Darryl sauntered off toward the small kitchen at the back of the cabin, leaving Michael alone with his thoughts.

Michael gritted his teeth. Only his brothers dared use that name; and even then, only when they wanted to drive him crazy. His lip curved when he remembered how Sheryl had called him Mikey when they first met. Either she had great instincts or some local had told her that name. He would have to remember to ask her sometime, he thought.

But first things first, he needed to speak to Connor about Roy and Exotic Rescue. He tried to catch the other man's gaze. Connor lifted his head, nostrils flaring as he picked up on the signal. Then with a nod of his head, he got up from his place on the cushion beside his wife and headed outside.

Connor was a tall burly man who was handsome in a hard sort of way. He was ex-military, and his entire carriage and bearing was testament to that. He had thick black hair which was slicked neatly back away from his face and even blacker eyes which were deep fathomless depths.

Michael had always felt closer to the other man, maybe because of their combined work in the Ops Unit. The pack had set up the covert military special ops of the Exotic Rescue and placed Connor in charge because he was ex-military and knew a thing or two about strategy and surveillance. In a mere thirteen months of existence, they had rescued twenty-three shifters from accidents and ambushes, and they had punished five sell-outs so severely that he doubted anyone was planning on betraying their kind any time soon. Connor had succeeded in building a fearsome image around the name of the Ops Unit and the few shifters who had had reason to know they existed had spread the rumors far and wide.

Not long ago, they had fingered the spy among their new recruits; a guy named Art Donahue had been feeding Roy information and Connor had put an end to that and tossed him out on his ear. But Michael couldn't shake the feeling that there was something they were missing. He couldn't say what it was, but he was almost certain there had to be another spy; well, either that or the horrifying idea that they got the wrong guy.

Michael frowned, marshaling his thoughts as he stared

off into the distance. He was generally the most strategic of the brothers and he had mad internet skills, but he was beginning to feel Roy was one-upping them in some way. Roy already knew about Tailan and it was a safe bet that he probably knew the exact location too. He realized then that he hadn't felt safe taking Sheryl back to Exotic Rescue because deep down he didn't trust everyone in Exotic Rescue.

"Something bothering you?" Connor demanded peering into Michael's face.

That was Connor; blunt and direct.

Michael nodded, "Exotic Rescue."

Connor's features sharpened with immediate interest, "I'm listening."

"A few weeks ago, we kicked out Art Donahue for working as a spy with Roy. He even admitted it when he said he hadn't meant to put Julia in danger," Michael began.

Connor's hands tightened into fists at this reminder of how Julia had been kidnapped. "Yes?" Connor demanded testily. "Why are we discussing this?"

"We don't need a reminder of Julia's kidnapping but stay with me for a minute. Ever since then Roy's managed to crown himself king of the vampires in exchange for promising them access to the Sunlight Ring."

"And?" Connor growled.

"Well, don't you find it strange that Art never went over to work with his 'former master' if truly Roy was it? Last I heard the guy left town so fast he was practically a blur. And don't you find it strange that we still have a few wire cuts, blank spots on security cams and inexplicable rise in death of sick shifters? I mean we lost three last week alone. Tailan doesn't fail but these days, it sure seems like… well, like it's failing. I mean unless someone is doing something to the supply those shifters are getting to make it less effective or something."

Connor frowned. And Michael knew he had his attention. That was the thing he loved about Connor. The man dealt with facts and when you presented him with cold hard facts, you had his attention.

"Yes, these things have happened in the weeks since Julia was rescued. But what do you think it means?" Connor demanded, watching Michael.

"It just occurred to me that we may have picked the wrong guy. Art Donahue didn't have enough intelligence and sly to be a spy. He might have confessed just to get you to stop beating the crap out of him or maybe he did it 'cos the real spy threatened him or something. I mean I don't know why he did it, but thing is, I'm willing to bet he isn't the spy."

Connor nodded, "That's some serious food for thought you've given me there. I didn't think you had it in you to be doing any thinking while you were closeted off with a beautiful woman in some wild forest getaway."

Michael rolled his eyes, "This was a hostage situation; just for her own good of course."

Connor's face adopted suitable gravity, "Of course."

Michael studied his face for any sign of teasing, but the other man didn't crack. He was deadpan.

Michael sighed. Sometimes with Connor, you just never knew. Even Theodore wasn't this hard to read. At moments like this he almost envied Darryl his mind reading skills.

Thinking of Darryl brought back the things Darryl had said about some frigid atmosphere between Sheryl and Hannah. He hadn't noticed it, but Darryl read minds, didn't he? He might be wise to listen to him.

If Sheryl had some problem with Hannah, she had given no sign and as far as he knew, there was no reason in the world why Hannah would have a problem with Sheryl. They had never met, and he and Hannah were history long before Sheryl came onto the scene.

Thinking of his relationship with Hannah left almost no taste in his mouth. They hadn't quarreled over some big betrayal or any such thing. They had simply... fizzled out. They had just realized they were more compatible as friends than lovers. There had been no spark, no nothing. Being with Hannah wasn't much different for him than being with one of the guys and it seemed she felt the same way. After trying very hard to make it work for a while, they had both agreed they had misread their relationship and they had gone back to being close friends and nothing more.

But Darryl was right in one thing though: he did have it bad for Sheryl. He would just have to let her know how he felt, he thought. This wasn't just sex for him; she was a very vital part of him, and he would let her know as soon as he got a chance to get her alone again.

Just then the front door flew open, and Julia strode out, her steps quick and urgent as she handed Connor his cellphone. "Quick. There's a call from Maria Henley."

Connor frowned. Maria was Theodore's Personal Assistant and Michael knew Connor had to be wondering, just like he was, why she was calling him rather than her boss.

"Connor speaking," Connor barked into the phone.

He listened for a minute, his gaze cutting to Michael's face. Then his expression turned cold and forbidding as he cut the call and faced Michael.

"Our home is under attack. We gotta move right now!" Connor barked.

Michael felt his heart sink. Only one person could be attacking Exotic Rescue right now; well, two actually: Roy or the spy Michael was certain was still planted somewhere in Exotic Rescue.

CHAPTER 11

One thing was clear to Sheryl as she watched the brothers strategize: this was a close-knit family bound together by love. Her gaze flicked to where Hannah stood off to the side, watching Michael with a half-smile that spoke of pride and longing playing about her lips and Sheryl ground her teeth as she amended: love and secrets.

What was the deal with that woman and Michael? He had said they were childhood friends but as far as she could tell they had chemistry that was hot enough to power a small volcano. True she hadn't caught any stray longing glances, but… a woman knew these things.

"Julia and Jessica will be safe here with Sheryl. Michael can stay and watch them," Theodore decreed.

"Absolutely not," Sheryl countered at the exact same moment with Jessica.

Both women shot each other surprised glances then exchanged smiles as Sheryl turned to face the men. "I've had enough of being cooped up in some strange cabin against my will. I'm getting out there today and no one is going to stop me."

Michael walked up to her and gathered her hands up in his. "We don't have time for this Sheryl. Roy is very dangerous. You need to stay right here and be safe while the rest of us go fix this."

She shook her head stubbornly.

He didn't let her get a word in as he plowed straight ahead, "Please just do as I'm asking. It's the only way I'll be able to concentrate."

Out of the corner of her eye, Sheryl couldn't help noticing Hannah standing close by and watching them.

As though she had noticed her quick glance in her direction, Hannah offered her own unwanted opinion, "Sheryl, he's right. You're only human which means you're not going to be able to defend yourself in danger like the other shifters would. Besides, Exotic Rescue isn't your home. It's theirs."

Sheryl turned to face her then, "I can take care of myself you know. Besides, this conversation is between me and Michael, so back off Hannah. Thank you."

The entire room fell silent, and all eyes turned to both of them. Sheryl saw Darryl give Michael a knowing look and she felt the look like a slap.

She grabbed Michael's hand, "Listen I know there is an emergency, and this isn't the time but there's something I need to speak to you about. In private."

He looked confused but he let her pull him along until they were standing outside beside the van everyone had pulled up in.

"How many times have you been intimate with Hannah?" she demanded.

"Sheryl!" he gasped.

"How many?" she demanded.

He sighed, "We had a relationship donkey years ago but that's over and done with. We're just friends now."

"Michael—"

"No forget it. I'm not giving you a number. What sort of man do you think I am? I would never betray Hannah like that," he declared, real anger rising in his eyes for the first time in her memory.

She studied him, studied the veins standing out on his neck in stark relief, studied the clenched fists. *Why is he so angry?* Sloan had adopted that same reaction the one time she had questioned him about something that looked like a lipstick mark on his shirtsleeve when she didn't wear any lipsticks that color.

Her heart thudded in her chest. Had she fallen in with another liar and cheater yet again? Was there some invisible sign on her forehead that said, 'Cheat on me?'

"You're not still dating her, are you?" she demanded.

Michael looked angry and disappointed all at once. "I don't believe this. Hannah and I were an item eons ago; of course, there is nothing more between us. For goodness' sake we ended things a whole three years ago. How could you possibly think such a thing of me? Notice I'm not grilling you about *Le Bastard*? Let it go Hannah, I don't like to talk about this right now," he added as he bent forward to place a distracted kiss onto her forehead.

Sheryl put up a hand like a traffic warden freezing him in place just inches before his lips touched her forehead. She gave him a death glare that could pulverize rocks as she announced, "Sheryl. My name is Sheryl."

"Crap. Slip of tongue—" he began.

"Was it?" she countered.

Then she turned and sauntered into the cabin without so much as a backward glance.

While Sheryl listened for the sound of the van leaving, she felt wooden and frozen and dead inside. He had called her Hannah. That just went to prove her point that something was up. Somehow, some way, she had ended up with a

Sloan in another skin and no matter how much she loathed admitting it to herself, she had gone and done the unthinkable: she had fallen for him.

The admission came with the relief one got after emptying a full bladder. She had commenced this trip to be rid of Sloan and all the bad memories that came with any thoughts of him. Yet somehow, she had ended up falling for Michael; except he was worse than Sloan because he wouldn't own up even when he had been caught.

After she had caught Sloan in the throes with Sally, she had blown her top and almost screamed herself hoarse from shock and pain and anger and an acute sense of betrayal. He had not bothered denying anything; but then again what was there to deny? She had seen them in living color, and she wasn't likely to forget that unfortunate encounter even if she went senile with age or something. Then as if it weren't bad enough, Sloan had had the unmitigated gall to order security to escort her out and he had tossed a pink slip in her face for good measure while he was at it.

In hindsight, she reflected that the pink slip had been unnecessary. She wasn't ever going to be able to work for him again anyway, pink slip or no. But the pink slip had rubbed salt on open wounds; telling her without words that he didn't regret his actions and he thought she could go to hell.

Firing her was a mistake and Kate had since then been champing at the bit to take his ass to court; but Sheryl didn't see the need. She had left New York behind and if she never saw Sloan or the city again it would be way too soon. Her entire belongings were packed into small, neat boxes and kept in storage, ready to be shipped over as soon as she found a place where she could settle down and start all over. And she *would* have a place already if a certain tawny-eyed Wolf shifter hadn't taken it upon himself to play Sir Galahad and kidnap her allegedly for her own good.

Thinking of Michael reminded her of the pain she had been keeping at bay and she realized for the first time that catching Sloan humping Sally paled in comparison to hearing Michael call her by another woman's name because his head was so wrapped around that other woman even if he wouldn't admit it.

Sloan's lie had left her enraged; Michael's left her hollow and hurt.

Michael's hurt more because she saw now that she had somehow fallen in love with him, and he had slipped into a part of her heart she wasn't even certain Sloan had ever entered.

With a sad glance at the kitchen door of the cabin where Julia and Jessica were making some pastries, she bypassed Hannah and Justin who were talking in hushed tones on the sofa beside the television. Justin had volunteered to stay with the women since Michael didn't want to miss the fight. He was a nice unassuming guy, a bit shy too. She couldn't be sure but for a minute there, Sheryl could have sworn she had seen a flash of longing in his eyes when he looked at Hannah. But it was gone as quickly as it appeared, and she shoved it from her mind.

Beside she had more pressing concerns— like getting off this mountain for one.

She spied a small notepad by the telephone, and she picked it up and tore off a sheet careful to pick up the pen lying beside the pad. She sat down and began to scrawl her note as fast as she could.

I have to go, Michael. I'm sorry. I know you only kept me here for my own good and I appreciate everything you've done for me. Sincerely. Thank you for keeping me safe all this while. But I see now that I was only getting in the way.

Forgive me.

Sheryl.

There! She was done. And she had managed to focus on the good things he had done and left out what she thought about him and Hannah.

But why was her vision getting blurry, she wondered with a frown. A great big splotch of wetness landed on the paper and then a second and then a third. She lifted a shaky hand to her eyes, and it came away wet. She was crying. She blinked in rapid succession to staunch the flow, but it wouldn't stop. With a grunt of dismay, she grabbed the note and hurried into the restroom, turning on the tap to dull the sounds and then she let herself slide onto the floor and let the tears come.

Sheryl couldn't escape the feeling of profound heartbreak. Her sobs were muffled but the pain could not be dulled; it sank into every fiber of her being with such intensity.

How could I have let Michael become so important to me in a matter of a few days? she wondered.

Her subconscious provided the answer: *Because, right from the onset, it had seemed almost as though we were meant to be. It had seemed almost as though fate had brought us together.*

They had similar likes and dislikes; they wanted almost the same things. Sometimes he could even anticipate her needs and what she was going to do next. He had given her laughter and fun and adventure because how did a reclusive kindergarten teacher end up in a jungle with a man who could become a Wolf? And she couldn't deny he had saved her life; those vampires would have … drunk her to death by now if he hadn't intervened.

But maybe they weren't meant to be together, like together. Maybe they were just like those proverbial ships passing in the night? They had impacted each other's lives but now it was time to move on. She knew she could never go back to teaching kindergarten; not after what she now knew about the real world that existed. She knew now that there was more to life than the books beneath her nose. She could never go back.

She could only go forward, but it seemed he wasn't destined to be part of her future beyond this point.

She would have to accept it, she thought, drying her tears with one hand while reading the note in her hand again. It had several splotches from tears, but she wasn't going to go through the stress of writing another one, she thought.

Her gaze lit on the small window high up in the bathroom wall, and her lips trembled as she recalled how she had shimmied out of the window in a bid to escape Michael the first day she was here. She smiled sadly now, recalling how proud she had been of herself for escaping him only to escape through the window to find him waiting for her as calmly as though it was the most normal thing in the world for her to arrive through the window.

A watery chuckle escaped her now as she recalled how shocked and frustrated, she had felt. In the space of a few days, she didn't recognize herself anymore. She had never been a wilting flower but for several years she had stopped being herself preferring instead to take the path of least resistance and to be self-effacing; until he had stormed into her life and reintroduced her to herself.

Now she recognized her strength for what it was: as asset. She liked to be assertive, strong, bold, and confident. She had noticed the same traits in Julia, Connor's new bride and she already admired the other woman immensely. Though she had to admit that when she thought about it, she didn't see Connor being with a woman who wasn't strong and self-assured. His pure alpha personality would override any woman who wasn't alpha and strong as all get out.

She had to leave, she decided, rising to her feet and placing the letter onto the sink and placing a soap on it to hold it in place. She headed for the window and climbed up easily before jumping out. This time, there was no Michael waiting for her, she noticed, feeling tears prick her eyes.

She dusted off her knees and hands and threw one last glance at the cabin. She felt her heart give a dull thud of pain. She had failed woefully in her bid to put the past behind her and love again. Michael could never be hers; not while Hannah still felt the way she did about him.

With a sigh, she turned and followed the bush trail, watching carefully where she was placing her feet. She didn't want to run into any snake thank you very much.

Her eyes were red-rimmed and swollen from sobbing so much and they hurt a little as she stumbled through the forest, trying to make as little noise as possible. She knew some vampires were still looking for her, but she hoped her paths and theirs would not cross. If she could just get back to her room in Susie Bones, she could check out, pick up her car and be out of Dodge in less than an hour.

"Stop right there," a strident feminine voice ordered from behind her.

Sheryl jerked to a halt and turned around. Hannah Walker was standing behind her, hands akimbo.

Sheryl cocked an eyebrow and waited.

"What do you think you're doing?" Hannah demanded.

"What does it look like? I'm leaving," Sheryl declared and turned to go.

Suddenly an invisible force yanked her right off her feet, lifted her straight into the air and smashed her into the ground.

"What the hell?" she yelled, jerking her frightened gaze to Hannah.

The other woman's hair was whipping straight out

behind her as though caught up in wind. For the first time Sheryl noticed that the hair was long enough to reach the backs of the other woman's knees. Hannah's hand was lifted straight out in her direction.

Sheryl tried to yank herself off the ground, but an invisible force held her pressed down to the ground.

"Michael wants you to stay right here so that's exactly what you'll do," Hannah declared.

"Like hell I will," Sheryl spat, trying to yank herself off the ground again.

A huge stone flew through the air and hit Hannah right in the back of her head with a frightening thunk. She went down without a sound, falling unconscious, and Sheryl yelped in horror even as the invisible force holding her down vanished.

"Witches can be a tiresome lot, don't you agree?" an amused, cultured voice announced.

Sheryl looked up with dread and felt all the blood drain from her face as she saw a familiar face grinning at her from beneath a cowboy hat. He was one of the men she had been spying on at Susie Bones. Michael said they were all vampires which meant they had found her.

His grin widened when he noticed her sudden pallor. "I see I need no introduction sweetheart. But just in case you didn't catch my name beneath all the 'nasty vampire' appellations, this here is Roy ma'am, at your service," he finished with a courteous bow that made her sick.

Sheryl rose to her feet, flicking Hannah a concerned glance. The other woman's chest rose and fell in small bursts of breath, and Sheryl felt a rush of gratitude. Hannah was still alive, she realized, releasing a gasp of relief.

"Don't rejoice too much, she'll soon be dead," Roy decreed motioning with his hands

Two vampires materialized, walking straight for Hannah

but when they tried to touch her, an invisible force slammed into their chests and they went down.

Roy's eyes widened like a child's staring at his favorite toy. "A powerful witch, ehh? You will come in handy my dear. Now I've decided that I want both of you," he decreed.

Sheryl saw with surprise that Hannah was already awake. She struggled into a sitting position and glared at Roy, "Stay away from us."

Roy tsked. "Guarding your little human rival for your boyfriend. Wow Hannah, your good works precede you," he mocked.

Hannah threw a small glance over her shoulder at Sheryl before enunciating, "Sheryl is no rival of mine. Whatever existed between Michael and I is long over. It's been over for three years."

"Except your heart doesn't agree does it?" Roy demanded in a silky tone. "I can hear your blood rushing through your veins, remember? I can hear how the flow speeds up when I mention Michael," he chuckled.

Sheryl threw Hannah a look, her heart sinking at this confirmation that her suspicions were correct.

Hannah's gaze met hers, "Don't believe what he says. He is a liar."

Sheryl broke the other woman's gaze, unable to bear the depth of supplication in those eyes. She held no grudges against Hannah. Michael was an amazing man; anyone would love him. She was the one who had come between both of them, but never again.

"You were attacking Exotic Rescue, weren't you? So how are you here?" Sheryl demanded.

Roy shrugged, "By the simple expedient of activating my mole. He's doing the attacking and I'm doing the reaping."

Sheryl's eyes widened in horror as understanding dawned, "He's not really attacking Exotic Rescue, is he? Just pretending to. All you wanted was a diversion so you could get me!"

He nodded in approval, "Very good. I see why the Wolf is so taken with you. Intelligent."

Sheryl's gaze went to Hannah again. The other woman had lost a lot of blood and was woozy. She couldn't be depended upon to join an escape plan. And they were several yards away from the cabin which meant Justin, Jessica and Julia wouldn't hear them even if they screamed.

She flicked Roy a glance again. He looked like just the sort of man who would harm anyone who stood in his way. Julia was pregnant and so was Jessica. The last thing she wanted was to get them out here where they could be hurt. It was better if she kept quiet, she decided, letting her eyes sweep the surroundings for a weapon. She saw nothing.

Roy shook his head, his eyes cold and lifeless as he warned, "If you try to escape, the witch dies."

CHAPTER 12

*R*oy Corning was a very happy man. Everything he wanted was within his reach. He knew those Exotic brothers would soon hand over his Sunlight ring with profuse apologies in exchange for the two captives he had now. Then he would weigh how important the human spy was to them. If she was really that important, he might come up with a strategy to use her to get some Tailan out of the brothers. Maybe he could convince them to get him a jar or something. Threaten them with her life or threaten to make her a vampire just like him. He chuckled aloud. Shifters hated vampires; they wouldn't like that.

Thinking of a whole jar of Tailan in his possession made his eyes kindle with a banked fire of greed burning in them. The mineral was nature's special gift to vampires as far as he was concerned. It wasn't meant for shifters. It was the one thing under the face of the sun that could let a vamp walk in daylight and his father had passed that precious secret on to him just before he died. Roy had precious few drops of the mineral left, he noted with a frown of displeasure which was why he had decided to use them to move around now so he could get what he wanted.

His lips curled in displeasure as he thought of his father's old concubine. The bitch wouldn't let him have her ring all those years ago, not even after he pleaded and promised to stay out of her way for the rest of his life. She wasn't a vampire which meant she didn't need it; but she was a witch which meant he couldn't compel it out of her. So, even though he had planned on approaching her now, cap in hand, after the Exotic brothers stole his ring, he had thought better of it. She hadn't agreed to help him all those years ago, she wouldn't do so now. She despised him so much he knew she wouldn't even spit on him if he were on fire.

He cast a thoughtful glance at Hannah where she sat in the corner, bound hand and legs with special ropes made from the Elderwood plant. That was the one herb capable of keeping a witch in check otherwise her magic would burst through the leaves unchecked. He had heard that every time a witch came near Elderwood it started shrieking and wouldn't stop. He was counting on the fact that these two women wanted to keep each other alive to please the Wolf and he sure hoped Hannah could help him make some headway getting that other ring from his father's concubine. He grinned; he wasn't sure what sort of getup they had going there but that Wolf, Michael, was one lucky dog. He would have to remember to get some tips from the man. No fighting, no rivalry, no jealousy: he kept two women and they protected each other at all costs to please him. Hmm.

Either Michael Bennet had mad fucking skills, or he had some ancient shifter secret up his sleeve. It would be interesting to get it, he thought, feeling his dick stir at the thought of getting his own Catrina to cooperate for a threesome if he found some other woman that took his fancy. Catrina was the most jealous of women, he thought with a sigh. But she satisfied him enough, so she was all right for now, he thought with a regretful glance at Sheryl's full thrusting breasts which were prominent beneath her small lace top.

Sean strode in just then, a short man with a crew cut and a perpetually bad temper. The weasel had learned to keep that foul temper in check around Roy because there could only be one boss around and only the boss could express feelings of anger to Roy's way of thinking. Anger was power after all; it was the one weapon his father had used to rule his world with an iron fist.

"Sean, where are Gary and Lloyd? They'll want to meet her," Roy said nodding in Sheryl's direction.

Sean shifted his foot. "They're still at the animal sanctuary boss. Gary says he needs to try get some vials of Tailan before he returns."

Roy observed Sheryl and Hannah watching him and he grinned. He was very satisfied with the absolute terror and disgust on their faces as they looked at him. Terror was good, disgust too. One only had to be able to enforce some things and one got what one wanted, he thought with a very satisfied sigh.

"Any dead shifters yet?" Roy demanded.

Sean shot the two women an uncomfortable glance and then looked away. His expression said that he felt uncomfortable spilling anything in front of those two.

Very good, Roy thought in approval. He had trained Sean well. And the man was human too. He knew Sean hoped he would turn him someday but that remained to be seen. He liked the other man just where he was: subservient and aware that with a flick of his hands Roy could break his neck and end him.

Catrina chose that moment to bustle into the room, her hands occupied with a tray laden with bags of blood. "Lunch is served," she called.

He grinned at her. She was dressed in see through fishnet from head to toe just like he wanted. She gloried in her near nakedness too, paying scant attention to the two women who were trussed up and sitting on the floor nearby.

He collected one bag of blood from her and pulled her onto his lap. "Yer a more preferable lunch, my darling," he drawled.

She giggled, just as he had expected her to. Boldly, he cupped one of her breasts in his hands, his breath hitching as his cock stirred. Catrina was already wet for him; he could smell her clean musky scent. He caught Sheryl watching them with absolute disgust stamped onto her features and he cocked an eyebrow at her.

"Don't give me that look. We both know yer not some vestal virgin."

The woman was no pushover. She shot back, "Virgin or not, I'm not given to wild animal lust right in the presence of witnesses. You want sex? Get a room."

"Look around. It's my home. I make the rules," he drawled testily.

"Well, I'm a guest in your home against my will I might add. Spare my eyes," Hannah spat, lending her voice to Sheryl's.

Roy chuckled. They were both little spitfires. Wow Michael *was* a lucky dog. With a nod at Sean, he said, "Bind the witch's eyes. Then get out of here."

Sean nodded and grabbed a blindfold. As he tied it onto Hannah's eyes, Sheryl fell silent. Satisfied that he had effectively silenced both women, Roy got to his feet, pulling Catrina with him and ignoring the tray of blood.

He drew her in for a long lingering kiss and when he released her, she whispered, "I love you."

"Come here and make me love you more. I want to fuck

you so hard that you won't be able to seat straight for days," Roy grunted grabbing the girl around the waist.

As Sheryl watched in horror, he sank his fangs into the girl's neck and began to suck her blood while she moaned in ecstasy. Catrina was used to his touch by now; she reveled in their own form of foreplay, he thought laving up some more blood and grinning as he caught Sheryl's horrified gaze.

"Don't look so judgmental honey. At least *I* don't use my powers to compel anyone's feelings," he taunted.

Sheryl frowned at him, "And what's that supposed to mean?"

"Don't listen to him," Hannah chided.

He effected a look of pretended shock, "Oh dear me. Didn't Mikey boy tell you his own unique abilities? Darlin' he can control emotions. So, all that mushy feeling in the pit of yer stomach? Fake! He can make you feel anythin' he wants you to feel any damn time. Yer just a puppet dancin' on the end of strings and he's the puppeteer," he finished with a nasty chuckle.

She turned satisfyingly white, and Roy chuckled some more. All in a day's work. No woman or man for that matter, liked to feel that their emotions had been controlled. They liked to know that they had their own free will every step of the way. He would leave her to reflect on his words for some time. Maybe in the end, she could even be his ally and then he wouldn't need to kill her or turn her. She would gladly become his bitch and help him bring down the Exotic boys from the inside.

Hmm, being a vampire had its perks, he decided as he carried Catrina in his arms and headed for his bedroom. He would suck and fuck her until he was sated. Then he would deal with his prisoners once and for all.

* * *

"Hannah. You're not asleep, are you?" Sheryl demanded in a low urgent whisper. She was still reeling from the information Roy had imparted but she didn't want to examine it too closely. Right now, she had a more pressing need: she needed to escape from this place and no way was she going without taking Hannah with her.

"I don't know what you think of me Sheryl, but I often need a comfortable bed to sleep in. Of course, I'm not asleep," Hannah drawled. "What are you planning?"

"How to escape, what else?" Sheryl demanded.

Hannah scoffed, "Who knows with you? You could be planning any number of things. I see Houdini has got nothing on you though. What's the escape plan this time?"

"What the hell does that Houdini crack mean?" Sheryl demanded.

Silence reigned a little then Hannah replied, "Why did you run from the cabin? Are you so determined to get Michael to hate me that you would run when you know he wanted me to keep an eye on you?"

Sheryl was taken aback at the conclusion Hannah had drawn. "Wow Hannah. You must think the world revolves around you. But can we maybe fight about this later? We got to move."

Hannah fell silent for a minute then she conceded, "I suppose you're right. So how do we do it? I can't see a thing cos that bastard blindfolded me and there's Elderwood on my bindings so I can't break free."

Sheryl chuckled without much sympathy, "You sort of had it coming with that whole 'do your worst' spiel you were dishing out. Come on use your mind to get the blindfold off. You're a witch aren't you and there's no Elderwood on that cloth, right?"

Hannah chuckled, "*He* had it coming. But yeah, I can at

least get the blindfold off," she murmured as she whispered some words and the cloth fell off her eyes.

Sheryl saw Hannah blink around as though trying to get her eyes to focus and she felt a tug of sympathy.

"See anything we can use to be free?" Sheryl asked. "Hurry."

Hannah looked around and then she started to shift her buttocks on the floor, pushing her body closer to the cold empty fireplace.

"What do you want to do?" Sheryl demanded, also mimicking Hannah and dragging her own buttocks along the floor.

Hannah chuckled. "You must have a lot of faith in me. You don't even know what I'm doing and you're following suit."

"Better than sitting around twiddling my thumbs," Sheryl averred.

Hannah reached the fireplace and turned around so her back was toward the grate and she could better reach it with her bound hands which had been tied behind her back. That was when Sheryl noticed the sharp jagged edge at the bottom of the grate, and she gave Hannah an approving grin. Hannah began to move her hands in an upwards and downward motion, obviously hoping to tear through the bindings with the sharp edge of the grate.

Within seconds, her hands sprang free, and she untied her legs and raced to untie Sheryl.

Sheryl gave a pleased sigh as her hands sprang free, "Well, if I had to be kidnapped along with anyone, I'm glad it was you."

Hannah gave her a half-smile that didn't quite reach her eyes. Sheryl wanted to ask her what was wrong but all of a sudden, all the hair at the back of her neck stood up in stark relief.

"I have a feeling we're about to get company," Sheryl whispered.

Hannah's eyes rounded. Then she sort of flicked her hands and an invisible force held the door down. Sheryl nodded in approval as they raced to the windows.

It was a very steep drop down to jagged rocks beneath that promised certain death.

"Any ideas?" she asked.

"I'm afraid my powers don't extend to flying," Hannah said shaking her head.

An urgent knock sounded at the door when whoever was at the other side couldn't open it.

"Hey! Hey! Open the door," the voice barked.

The women exchanged glances and Hannah grinned, "They can try forever. They won't open that door until I lift the curse I placed on it."

"When will you lift it?" Sheryl asked, feeling her heart squeeze with a little fear at this information that Hannah could place curses. She *was* a witch then.

Hannah gave Sheryl a serene smile, heedless of her inner turmoil, "I'll lift it when the sun turns green at noonday."

Sheryl grappled with that in her mind and then frowned, "Which means never?"

Hannah shrugged.

Sheryl ran to grab the drapes to make some sort of makeshift escape rope and when she tugged at them, she upended a table beside the curtain and a jar of golden liquid spilled out. Sheryl stared at it in shock and started to reach for it, mesmerized by its appearance.

Hannah suddenly appeared beside her just before her hand touched the substance and kicked her hand away.

"Ow."

"That's Tailan. It can burn human skin like acid." So,

saying she reached down and touched it and carried it to her nose and perceived it. She nodded in confirmation.

"Why doesn't it burn your skin?"

"Because I'm part Fae and a healer," Hannah said. "I'm not human."

Sheryl's eyes strayed to where some rings very much like Roy's former ring were contained in a little transparent box which had fallen along with the Tailan. She frowned. "I've seen this ring before."

Hannah nodded, "It all makes sense now. My God it all makes sense now. Those are pure ruby rings, and he concentrates them using Tailan. That's how he walks in the sun."

Sheryl looked at Hannah. "We have to get out of Dodge now."

The woman raced to the window and started to drop the curtain when suddenly a great big dragon, screeched past.

Hannah's eyes widened in disbelief. "That's Connor."

Sheryl couldn't believe her eyes. The dragon was even bigger in real life than it had seemed in movies. He spotted them and headed straight for them, wings flapping.

"Are you sure? Isn't he at Exotic Rescue?" Sheryl asked, afraid to hope. She couldn't bear any disappointment just now. She just wanted to see Michael's face one last time before anything happened to her and if this dragon turned out to be maybe some other dragon Roy had in his employ, she knew she wouldn't be able to stand the shattered hope.

Hannah shook her head, brimming with confidence, "I can pick Connor out of a thousand dragons. That's him all right."

Her confidence calmed Sheryl and yet put her on edge. Hannah knew the entire family and got along with them in a way she could never hope to.

"Besides Michael's pretty damn smart," Hannah continued. "He must have seen the incident at Exotic Rescue for the smoke screen it was and changed direction at once."

"Michael isn't with him," Sheryl pointed out.

"That's Connor," Hannah decreed in a voice that brooked no argument.

The dragon reached them and suspended a bit lower than the window and waited.

"What's he doing?" Sheryl demanded.

"Getting us out of Dodge," Hannah said.

She shoved Sheryl onto the dragon's back and followed while the sound of pounding and threats continued on the door Hannah had spelled.

The dragon leapt, with grace, into the air and Sheryl screamed in exultation. "This is better than a private jet."

Hannah said nothing more but gave her a bright smile in response, that made her look breathtakingly beautiful.

Sheryl felt her heart constrict in her chest as she beheld the smile. How in the world was she expected to compete for a man's attention with such a woman?

She loved Michael, she thought admitting the truth she had known for a while but never thought out loud. But so did Hannah, and Hannah had him first. Sheryl could bet her entire life's savings that Hannah still loved Michael and she wouldn't be wrong. Hannah was calm, serene, unassuming and maddeningly beautiful. She wanted to hate the other woman but, how could she? Hannah had done her no wrong, and heck, she was the reason she had escaped Roy's clutches.

It was high time she admitted another truth that had been right in front of her face from the get-go: Michael would never be hers.

CHAPTER 13

Michael couldn't stop pacing. Try as he might, he couldn't stop wearing a path into the carpet with his continuous pacing back and forth. He wanted to know what had happened with Sheryl, but he couldn't find out.

They had arrived Exotic Rescue to find half the security team missing and the other half strung up. Kids had been running amok and so had shifters and animals. They had prepared immediately to engage only to discover a wild monkey had been let loose on the ground and in the chaos that followed, half the security men had left their posts to try to coral it while the other half that remained had been overpowered and strung up. A quick search through the grounds and especially in the location of Tailan had revealed no impostors. Heck even the tied-up security men had said the men who tied them up had driven off laughing.

He had known at once that the real target had to be Sheryl. He hadn't had a moment's peace since then. And just as he was realizing it, a frantic Jessica had called from the cabin to report that Hannah and Sheryl were missing. His entire world seemed to have been turned upside down in the space of a few minutes. He was beside himself with worry, unable to stand anything or anyone else and he had been impossible to placate.

He had wanted to charge straight to Roy's but Connor, cold calculative leader that he could be sometimes, had felt he was too emotionally attached to be counted on to be professional and detached. Connor had convinced him when he had gotten through to him with the argument that Sheryl could die if he made a mistake.

So, he had returned to the cabin on tenterhooks and almost killing himself with worry. A tearful Julia had shoved the note they had found in the bathroom into his hands, and he had realized the note was covered in tears.

Julia had shaken her head at once as though reading his silent enquiry. "Those aren't my tears. Hannah must have seen it when she went to use the restroom and gone after her to get her back and then Roy must have captured them both."

His hands had been shaky as he sank onto the nearest cushion, not trusting his legs to support his weight. He had waited in vain for the shaking to stop and it hadn't; not even after Jessica had thrust a glass of iced tea into his hands. Julia had begun assuring him that Roy wasn't so bad as to harm Sheryl after all he had kidnapped her himself and let her escape. Julia had even offered to go help Connor find Sheryl since Julia herself could also fly. Julia was a Fox shifter, but she was also an absorber which meant she could absorb other shifters' abilities. She had absorbed her husband's flying skills and that had saved her when Roy had kidnapped her a few weeks ago.

But his Sheryl couldn't fly, and neither could Hannah. If anything happened to Sheryl, he knew he wouldn't be able to go one living. He couldn't —

Just then he heard the great big flapping of wings that

signaled Connor's return and he sped to the door of the cabin. He was so excited that he didn't even wait to open it; he burst right through the door, leaving a Michael-shaped hole where it had once stood.

His eyes blazed with relief when he saw Sheryl and Hannah climbing off Connor's back and before he could stop himself, Michael had catapulted across the space separating them and hefted Sheryl into his arms. She was amazingly beautiful, and she was all his. He caught her up in his arms, screaming in delight as he turned her around and around in circles, rejoicing and exulting in her warm, vibrant being. She was safe. She was safe. He placed her back onto the floor and swooped down on her lips with a kiss so exuberant and passionate that they might as well have been alone. He spied Jessica wiping emotional tears from her eyes as she stood watching them. Connor had also changed back into human form and was busy with his own wife.

Michael's emotions were too intense. He needed to be in his Wolf form because he couldn't control the intense emotion searing through his Wolf again. He yanked his lips from Sheryl's and morphed into his Wolf form and he bounded around the perimeters of the compound in joy.

Sheryl cut a glance at him, confusion stamped into her pretty features. He saw Hannah lean toward her and explain, "He cannot contain his joy that you returned to him alive. He can only better express himself in his Wolf form."

After he had tired himself out running, he ran back to her, changed back to human form and kissed her again, deep and hard. He wanted to brand her as his, he realized. She was his mate for life, but he wanted to put his own particular mark on her.

As though she had read his thoughts, she became stiff and uncomfortable in his arms. Belatedly, he realized she wasn't very comfortable with his family yet and realized the show of emotion might have put her off a little.

"I have never been so happy to see anyone in my entire life," he told her, sincerity throbbing in his voice. "I'm sorry if I embarrassed you just now. I'm just so relieved that you're all right. I even went to Susie Bones and picked up your clothes and belongings."

Her eyes brightened.

Encouraged he continued, "I was so desperate and eager for anything that reminded me of you because if I could sniff your clothes and hold your fragrance in my heart, I could pretend you were close by. I even picked up your car and it is at Exotic Rescue now just raring to go."

The light in her eyes dimmed.

What had he said wrong now?

Then she gave him an overly bright smile that was so plastic it was almost hard to watch as she patted his cheek and said, "I'll check if I have anything else in the cabin. Then I'll be ready to leave."

She walked around him, giving him a wide berth and headed into the cabin.

Hannah gave him a swift kick in the shin, "How could you be so obtuse?"

He frowned. "Huh?"

"Come with me, you giant oaf," she ordered and jerked him away from Connor and the rest, leading him off into the trees.

He didn't notice Sheryl watching them with a sad smile from a cabin window.

As soon as they reached the shelter of some trees and were out of earshot, Hannah spat, "Are you trying to lose her?"

"What are you talking about?" he sputtered.

"Why are you being an ass? She's been so eager to see you and first thing you tell her is that her car is ready?"

He frowned. "Well, it is."

He barely escaped another kick aimed at his shin.

"Okay stop kicking me and tell me what's wrong," he demanded, both hands out in a classic sign of surrender.

"Do you love me?" Hannah demanded.

Michael winced. "Of course not. Where did that come from? I mean I love you as a friend but nothing more. Come on Hannah, we both agreed that we were better as friends, 'cos there was no other spark between us."

And she chuckled though the sound seemed a bit sad and regretful to him. "I thought so. Well, Sheryl is convinced we love each other and she's getting in the way."

"Where would she get a crazy idea like that?" he thundered.

Hannah rolled her eyes at him, "Charming as always. Well, I know you didn't mean to insult me, so I'll let that slide. Point is, go talk to her."

Michael frowned some more, "I just talked to her."

"No, you mauled her in front of everyone like all you had going for you two was sex. But I see the way you look at her Michael. You never looked at me like that in all our years of friendship."

Was it his imagination or had her voice trembled a little over that last sentence?

"I think you love her," Hannah concluded.

"Of course, I do," he spat. "Was there ever any doubt?"

Hannah shrugged, "Plenty. On her part."

He frowned, "How did you know?"

She sighed, "I saw her note Michael. It was simple and heartfelt but…"

His heart was in his throat, "But what?"

"It was covered with wet splotches Michael. Those were

tears of heartbreak. I didn't like her at first because I thought she was just one of those big city types come to take advantage of your goodness. But when I saw those tears, I knew she had fallen in love with you."

Michael swallowed past the lump of regret in his throat. "She seems to be doing a lot of crying these days. At least ever since she met me."

Hannah said nothing else, she simply towed him along again in the direction of the cabin. Sheryl was just coming out of the cabin, her steps unhurried.

"I think I've gotten everything now," she told him.

He looked at her and for the first time noticed that the incredible sadness he had seen in her eyes that first time in the gas station was back. With a jolt he realized that through the period of kidnapping her, making love to her and being cooped up with her in the cabin he had seen anger, tears, rebellion, laughter, happiness and so much else in her eyes, but never that heartbreaking sadness.

He swallowed with difficulty as he said, "I need to talk to you Sheryl."

She looked from him to Hannah. "I doubt there's anything left to say. Except perhaps heartfelt thanks to Hannah and Connor. They saved my life."

He grabbed her hand just like Hannah had done with him and towed her toward the cabin. Justin, Connor, Jessica, Julia and Hannah wisely remained outside, loading up the van to leave.

Michael stole a glance at Sheryl. The tables had flipped indeed. The first day his family had come here, she had been nervous around them where she had been free with him. But today, she was warm and generous around his family but stilted and formal with him.

He led her to a cushion and sank down beside her.

He took her hand, forcing her to meet his gaze.

"I haven't been very predictable since we met. I've taken you out of your way against your will—"

"You did it to protect me," she told him woodenly as though she were reading her part in a script.

"I didn't let you contact your family," he continued, determined to place the litany of all his sins on the table.

"You were protecting them," Sheryl replied in that same wooden tone, still defending him.

"I took you away from your comfortable hotel room and brought you here. And then I turned into a Wolf and tricked and frightened you into not leaving."

"You did what you had to."

"I didn't tell you about Hannah even though we're through, and then I made love to you," he whispered, emotions making his voice raw.

She had no comeback for this one. She merely looked away and he was afraid she was hiding tears.

"I allowed myself develop feelings for you and I think you also have the same feelings for me," he said.

She turned to face him, anger blazing in her eyes as she retorted. "I had no feelings for you. You forced those feelings on me."

Michael was taken aback. "What?"

"It's true. I know your dirty little secret," she spat climbing to her feet, every fiber of her being vibrating with rage.

Michael frowned as he too rose to his feet, "I have no secrets from you."

"Sure, you don't. You just forgot to mention—"

"Me?" Hannah asked, walking inside.

Both their faces turned to her. Hannah flicked her eyes to Sheryl's ravaged face and intoned quietly, "Listen to me Sheryl. I'm a woman like you so we should understand ourselves. I would never lie to protect him if this isn't the absolute truth. Michael and I ended things three years ago by mutual agreement. We just stayed friends because we've always been friends since childhood."

Sheryl shook her head in denial, "I see how you look at him."

"And I see how he looks at *you*," Hannah countered. "It's true for a moment there, I thought we could get back together but only out of force of habit. I felt we had both been single for three years so perhaps we ought to give it another shot. That's all."

Sheryl didn't look convinced. "You weren't happy when you saw me here at first."

Hannah didn't deny it, "I thought you were one of those shallow women from the city who would only try to take advantage of his goodness. But I've watched you try to save me from Roy in the forest even when you thought I was your rival. I've seen your strength and undaunted courage. I've seen how you handled your fears and doubts with maturity and selflessness. You were even ready to sacrifice your love for me. You're a good person Sheryl and I know Michael needs you. Please don't drag me into the equation. I was never in it."

Michael looked at Sheryl, "Please. She's telling you the truth. I love you. I love you with all my heart. I want to spend the rest of my life with you."

Sheryl looked a bit shocked at his declaration. Her eyes scanned his face as though assessing his sincerity. He let his emotions show on his face, his eyes burning with intensity as he let her look into his soul.

Sheryl was the most important person in his life. She was all that mattered to him. She made him whole. He needed her desperately. He knew she loved him as much as he loved her. He had seen it in her tears and her moans of pleasure when she was in his arms, and her selflessness, and her unspoken need to always have him near, and her quiet pride in him, and how she made him feel like the king of the whole damn world. He had seen the trust shining from her eyes when she looked up at him as he plunged into her tight wet pussy. He had seen her quiet contentment in sleeping near him. He needed her but she needed him too. She needed to be free of her hang-ups with *Le Bastard* and whatever pain he had inflicted on her.

Sheryl bit her lip as though thinking then she said the last words he expected to hear, "There's more. There's another more important reason why I cannot be with you. And Michael, you won't change my mind."

CHAPTER 14

Sheryl could feel the tiny ripple of shock that accompanied her announcement. It flowed from Michael to Hannah and back. She saw them exchange glances. She knew now that there was nothing more between them because no woman alive would lie like that in order for her man to be with someone else.

Or would she, she wondered, eyeing the lingering sadness in the depths of Hannah's gaze.

Refocusing her mind on her goal, she let her eyes return to Michael's features. His expression was closed and shuttered as though he she had reached across the space separating them and slapped him.

"Sheryl? What are you saying?" he demanded closing the gap separating them physically.

He could never close the emotional gap now though, she thought. It yawned like a chasm between them.

She took a step back, creating more physical distance of her own as she said, "Your abilities."

He frowned, "You already know I'm a shifter. Come on

that's no problem. Jessica is human, Theodore is a shifter, and they are happy."

Her heart thudded in her chest, "W-Why bring that up? They are married."

He grinned happily, "So? It's what I want too if you want it. The whole nine yards. Together forever," he said.

Out of the corner of her eyes, she spied his siblings edging closer and trying to look nonchalant about it. She turned to look at them. Connor and Justin looked so hopeful. Jessica and Julia were already high fiving each other. Only Hannah was watching her with some measure of wariness as though she could sense some more turbulence beneath the surface.

That's right, Hannah was a healer which meant she had to be more attuned to emotions than the rest.

Sheryl thrust out her chin and turned to face Michael. "I know you're a shifter. I didn't know though that you could control emotions."

He blanched.

Roy had been right, she thought, her heart twisting as though a knife had been thrust into her chest. "How do I know you didn't control my alleged feelings for you? How do I know any of this is real?"

He grabbed her shoulders and gave her a small shake, looking devastated and shattered, "Sheryl, how could you even conceive such a despicable thing?"

She flung off his hands, getting worked up now that they were on the subject. "Very well. Go on, lie and say you've never used your powers to control how I feel."

He opened his mouth to speak at once, then, obviously, a memory struck, and he fell silent.

Sheryl shook her head in disgust. "That's what I thought."

"Sheryl, wait—" he tried.

"I don't want to hear it. You toyed with my feelings and made me feel things that weren't there."

His siblings were all thronged around them now. Connor was already shaking his head in denial of her words and in defense of his brother. What had she expected? Sympathy? Honesty? Understanding?

She would always be an outsider to these people; perhaps an outsider without feelings. They didn't expect her to be hurt by their antics.

"How could you do this to me? You knew about *Le Bastard*. You knew I walked in on him cheating on me and you know that must have affected my ability to trust anyone, but I trusted you anyway. How could you toy with my emotions?"

"Sheryl—" he tried again in a voice that seemed broken.

She held her tears at bay as she spat the words at him overriding his words, "I don't know what gave you the right to think you could play God with my feelings. First you grabbed me and took me where you wanted because you decided I was safer that way. Did you also make me fall in love with you because you decided I was safer that way? And the lovemaking? Was that a lie too? Did I really want to make love, or did you make me think I wanted to? What was I? Just some human you needed to screw in every sense of the word so you could prove to yourself the extent of your shifter abilities? Say something damnit!"

He gave her an icy glare as he stepped backwards, "I'll say this to you just this once, so listen. I only used my powers once to calm you down when you were upset. But that you could even think such horrible things about me... I don't know what I was thinking," he finished shaking his head as he took a few more steps backwards separating himself even more than before.

Sheryl looked at the space between them and felt pain swell in the region of her heart.

Well, wasn't this what you wanted, her subconscious chided without sympathy.

No, it wasn't, her heart cried, splintering into a million pieces at the keening sense of loss.

She had hoped he would tell her it was all a lie that Roy had lied. She had needed to hear the words from his lips but instead he had acted as though she had committed some heinous crime. He had clamped up and shut her out and thus confirmed her worst fears.

Without another word, Michael spun around on his heel and stalked off without a backward glance.

Sheryl made to leave too when Connor's quiet voice interrupted, shaking with rage, "I don't know what makes you think you can just leave."

She quirked a brow, "Excuse me?"

"The vampires still have a kill order on you. Perhaps more so now than before. And you and Hannah are yet to be debriefed. So, Ms. Quinn, I'm afraid you'll have to avail yourself of our hospitality for some more extended period of time."

She gave him a dirty look, all her gratitude at his help in saving them dissipating like a candle in the wind. "And if I refuse?"

He didn't answer. He just threw a glance over his shoulder. At once, Justin, whom she had liked as quiet and reserved stepped forward, handcuffs dangling from his fingers.

Sheryl gave the cuffs a horrified look. She had never been cuffed in her entire life. She looked over at where Michael had clambered into the driver's seat, but he wouldn't even look at her. He stared straight ahead as though she had ceased to exist.

Bitterly she thrust both hands forward, "Thank you for disabusing me of all notions that I was anything more than your captive."

Connor's voice far exceeded hers in iciness as he retorted, "Thank you for being a model captive and reminding us of our evil roles."

As she was hauled away to the waiting van, she heard Jessica murmur to Connor in a troubled voice, "What are you doing? Theodore won't like this."

Connor growled. "You're right. He would prefer I had strapped her to the back of the van and hauled her all the way home. Hung, drawn and quartered the medieval way."

"Connor—" Julia tried.

"Not now Julia," he snapped. "She wounded Michael. I can take anything but not seeing someone hurt Michael so brutally after he saved her scrawny little ass."

Sheryl mimicked Michael and stared straight ahead, presenting them with her proud unbending profile. She didn't deign to say anything to anyone all the way to Exotic Rescue.

When they reached the much talked about sanctuary it was all she could do to maintain her detached mien. Exotic Rescue was quite an establishment. If she hadn't been warned beforehand that it was an animal sanctuary, she would have thought it was a resort. It had rows and rows of palm trees and exotic looking flowers lining different areas of the sanctuary. It had rolling fields of greenery for miles in every direction doted by pockets of lush, bright colored flowers nodding their tender heads in the wind. Coconut trees disappeared down a winding path toward what seemed to be a beach. The property spread out with no end in sight, with dotted towering buildings scattered in artful disarray all around. There was a row of rough, jagged mountains that served as a backdrop to the picturesque location and there were even small barb-wired enclosures that held animals. The sweet smell of nature assailed her senses, and she inhaled deeply, feeling every inch of her body relax in automatic response.

It was sheer beauty and luxury. Whoever had built this resort was sensuous and a student of luxury. Her eyes landed thoughtfully on Jessica. She was married to Theodore, wasn't she? As though she had heard her thoughts, Jessica grinned and gave her a small wink.

Only then did Sheryl remember to jerk her gaze away and pretend disinterest.

She was helped down from the van by Justin while Michael remained behind the wheel exuding impatience as though he had somewhere else to be. Connor helped his wife and Jessica down and led them away toward some high-rise buildings that she assumed were their lodgings or something.

She let Justin lead her away to what she expected to be the dungeon but as soon as they passed the huge glass doors, she knew it couldn't possibly be.

The elevator took them straight up to the penthouse and Justin led her to what turned out to be a conference room. As she entered, she saw the room already occupied by Theodore, Jonathan, and Darryl. There were also two men in the room whom she didn't know. One was elderly while the second was younger and exuded an air of restrained danger.

Their eyes all locked on the cuffs at once and a thunderous frown appeared on Theodore's face as he demanded, "Justin! Explain!"

Just two words but they were enough to make the younger man shuffle his feet like a teenager. He unshackled the cuffs with satisfying haste and took them off her, but Theodore was not appeased. He had risen to his feet, his eyes a storm as he waited for the explanation he had demanded. Obviously, he wasn't the sort to repeat himself.

One look at his face and Sheryl felt a rush of sympathy for poor Justin. She angled herself slightly in front of him as though to protect him as she announced, "I felt frustrated at having to come here again rather than being released to go home. I demanded they treat me as the prisoner I obviously was rather than pretending hospitality, and Connor had the bright idea to use the cuffs."

Theodore glared at poor Justin and then folded his hands as though waiting for someone. Sheryl understood at once that he was waiting for Connor and she continued in a smooth tone, "Connor may be a while. He is helping your wife and his to their lodgings."

"Is he now?" Theodore demanded in a silky tone that was hard to read.

Is he trying not to laugh?

"He didn't do anything wrong either," Sheryl continued, defending Connor in spite of her anger at the man. "He was just frustrated because he felt I had treated his brother in an unfair manner."

She could understand his need to protect his younger brother. Kate would have reacted in pretty much the same way, she realized.

Theodore's eyes cut to her face as his frown began to ease. His lips even quirked a little as though he were fighting back humor as he demanded, "And did you?"

The door opened just then behind her and even without turning around, she knew one of the two footsteps she heard was Michael's. He only had to walk into a room and every cell in her body responded, every fiber of her being went on high alert and she became a quivering mass of want and need and longing.

In a clear voice that carried a faint thread of an apology beneath it, she conceded, "I may have made some unfair accusations when I spoke to Michael."

She felt Michael's gaze whip to hers, so she clarified, "I wasn't totally wrong, but perhaps I carried it a bit too far. And that's all I'm going to say on the subject," she added.

She thought she heard Michael curse under his breath, *Damned spoiled New Yorker.*

Theodore nodded in response to her last statement, "Fair enough."

And he too returned to his seat. As though that was the signal they had been waiting for, everyone else also returned to theirs. She saw now that it was Hannah who had come in with Michael. She waited to feel that same hollow jealousy, but she felt nothing, and she knew she had really come to terms with their friendship.

What did it matter if she had or had not? She and Michael were over and done with. They were finished. He couldn't prove to her that he hadn't used his powers to influence her feelings for him and she couldn't prove it to herself either.

There was nothing left to say.

"These are Drake and Joshua Cox. They are shifters from Weirna, a neighboring town and they are friends," Theodore said, introducing the two men she hadn't recognized. Both men gave her small bows of greeting and she nodded in response.

"We apologize for your less than restful vacation Sheryl," Jonathan began in a quiet voice. "We acknowledge that we were largely to blame."

Sheryl was surprised. Theodore was the leader and she had expected him to lead but Jonathan had. Well, at least *someone* with some sincerity acknowledged their role in the upheaval her life had undergone in less than five days.

She shrugged.

"We would like to compensate you for your trouble and find some safe house for you away from this city if you're loathe to stay here with us until this blows over," Jonathan continued. "Vampires can be a persistent lot so we have every reason to believe you may still be in danger were we to simply leave you to your own devices. And then," he added with a small glance at Michael, "We wouldn't be able to forgive ourselves."

It was clear to see that Jonathan was the peacemaker of the bunch, she thought and their negotiation specialist. She saw the cheque lying in front of him and suspected he was about to hand it over.

She faced Theodore, "Boy you must really want to avoid that lawsuit."

It was his turn to shrug.

She continued, "Well, keep your cheque. Hannah and I think we may have found out how Roy makes those Sunlight Rings of his."

All eyes fastened onto her face at once and dead silence reigned in the room.

She threw Hannah a glance and Hannah gave her an encouraging nod.

"He used Tailan," she continued.

Ripe curses swept the entire room, and the brothers upended their chairs as they all began to pace and curse and stamp about. Only Jonathan, Joshua and Michael remained seated. Even Drake was very vocal in cursing and punching walls.

When the male sounds had died down some, Michael spoke to her for the first time since their argument, "Are you sure? How do you know it was Tailan?"

She shrugged, "I don't. Hannah identified it. But I sure as hell know my jewelries as any spoiled New Yorker should," she added, careful not to look at Michael.

He shifted in discomfort at that pointed barb, and she continued with satisfaction, "And I know ruby and those rings were pure ruby. So, they're obviously mixing them with this Tailan thing in some way to be able to walk in sunlight."

Theodore's voice shook with rage as he declared, "I'm going to kill Roy with my bare hands. So, it's been about Tailan all along? That's why first Atlas and now Roy have been after Exotic Rescue."

"His loyal moronic human followers are in it for the money though. I've questioned a few and even they have no clue what the real deal is," Connor chipped in.

Sheryl frowned, she hadn't noticed when he had entered.

Did he always move so silently? Boy, he must be good at that tracking stuff, she thought.

With a sigh she faced Theodore, "I don't think even his vampires know how he gets those rings. When I was spying on them at Susie Bones all he told them was that the substance was very rare and very expensive, but Theodore Cooper would pay for it."

Theodore straightened, "Oh someone *will* pay for Roy's actions. But it won't be Theodore Cooper. Please escort Miss Quinn to her lodgings, Hannah," he said, dismissing both of them.

Sheryl rose and walked to the door. Hannah caught up with her and they both left the room.

Sheryl looked at the other woman. She seemed too serious in her opinion and somewhat withdrawn. She had decided she liked Hannah and she didn't want them to leave things on a sore note especially after they had helped each other over at Roy's.

With a maddening grin, she gave Hannah a slight poke with her elbow as she teased, "Think they were checking out our asses as we left?"

Hannah blanched, "God I hope not. There isn't much to see in mine," she deadpanned as she indicated her rather small backside.

Sheryl whooped with delighted laughter. The sound seemed to have attracted attention and a door farther down the hall opened. Jessica poked out her head and grinned, "I thought that sounded like you. No one else would dare to laugh in Teddy's hallowed halls."

Sheryl grinned at the friendliness on the other woman's face. "Come on. Not even you, his wife?"

Jessica grinned demurely, but Sheryl caught the impish light in her eyes as she confessed, "With Theodore, there isn't much I won't dare."

Sheryl had a feeling that was true. The pair complemented each other so well. If only she and Michael…

"Come in for some lemonade both of you," Jessica invited in a voice that brooked no argument and interrupted Sheryl's train of thought.

As soon as Hannah and Sheryl entered the office, Sheryl caught sight of Julia sitting on one of the soft cushions in the homey room. She suspected at once that Jessica had been actively listening for them. This wasn't in the least accidental.

As Jessica poured the lemonade, Julia asked questions about their findings at Roy's. Following Hannah's lead, Sheryl shared the information. She didn't think Theodore and Connor would keep it from their wives anyway.

As they sipped lemonade and exchanged girl talk, the conversation came around to her and Michael as she had known it would.

Sheryl started to shake her head, her eyes stern, as she tried to head them off.

Julia's soft voice overrode her unspoken protest, "I've been thinking about where you could get such an idea that Michael had used his powers to influence your feelings and then I remembered you had been with Roy."

Her quiet words snapped Sheryl to attention.

Julia continued, "I see my suspicions were right. Roy planted those thoughts in your head, didn't he? Well, Roy may not have told you, but he is a lifelong enemy of the brothers and there's no one he hates more than Theodore and Michael."

"Roy made me believe Theodore was conducting experiments on helpless animals," Jessica said. "I almost broke up with him until I learned the truth."

"And he made me believe Connor was vicious and violent. I ran away," Julia supplied.

Sheryl's eyes widened as understanding dawned, "So you think he..."

"Yes Julia. Think of him as the Satan in your Garden of Eden story," Hannah chipped in. "I've known Michael for years and he let me leave him because I didn't love him anymore. He could have used his abilities in such a manner, but he would never abuse his powers. Come on you know him. Isn't he good, and pure and a perfect gentleman? Do you really think him capable of such despicable acts?"

No, I truly don't, Sheryl realized.

Hannah wasn't done. "Another thing you should know, you were both always fated to happen. I sense these things. Didn't something unusual happen when you met?"

Unusual? Sheryl squinted and shrugged as she narrated the story at the gas station.

"The pigeon was unusual," Hannah pointed out. "It hopped from you to him along an invisible cord connecting both of you. This is fate. Can you deny that he's been a perfect gentleman all this while?"

"Apart from when he's kidnapping women from their hotels—" Jessica supplied.

"And even then, for their own good," Julia finished.

Sheryl couldn't take anymore. She burst into tears.

CHAPTER 15

*H*e wanted to stay angry at Sheryl. I want my anger to last me a lifetime and help me get over her and forget her, Michael thought, still burning with anger as he stared off into the distance, waiting for Theodore and the others to emerge. But try as he might, every time he closed his eyes, he saw her face. He saw her laughing up at him, he saw her tearing up when he had been a jerk, he saw her yelling at him. He saw her every time, period. It is driving me crazy, he thought with a vicious oath.

He could still remember how she had shielded first Justin and then Connor from Theodore's wrath even though she must have still been upset at the way they had treated her. She had managed to take all the blame on herself and she had managed to make it seem as though they were totally justified.

Justin couldn't sing her praises enough since then and Michael understood why. She was pure dynamite.

Well, he was going off with his brothers to teach Roy a lesson. Once they were back, he would drive her to the border of town himself and make sure she got out safe, then he would return home and just forget about her.

This time the snarl from his wolf was so strong he felt a tingly, as if it would take him over right then and there and release a howl to end all howls.

He struggled to contain it. He didn't have the luxury of feelings. He had to forget about her.

He was frustrated he thought. How could someone love someone so much and yet be so wrong about them? How could she believe such despicable things about him?

As though he had conjured her with his thoughts, she came walking toward him. He kept his expression blank as he asked, "Did you need me for something?"

She nodded and kept coming until she was a hair's breadth away. Her eyes sparkled as she looked up at him and confessed, "I've been a fool and an idiot. I'm very sorry, Michael."

He lifted an eyebrow in silence and waited.

Sheryl looked down at her hands. "I accused you of some pretty serious stuff and made it clear that I didn't trust you. Sure, I had my baggage from the past, but... you're nothing like Sloan."

That was the first time he was hearing the name. "I take it Sloan is *Le Bastard*?"

She nodded unhappily. "He did a number on me, but you didn't deserve any of that. I shouldn't have believed Roy when he implied that you had used your powers on me. I... I shouldn't have believed him. I get why you're so mad at me. I deserve it. I shouldn't have said those things to you. I was wrong. Can you forgive me?"

Michael stared at her, his heart lifting in his chest. He couldn't help himself. She knew how to own up to her faults and she didn't try to duck responsibility for them. He loved her like crazy but the things she had said... she had some serious trust issues. And while he owed Roy a black eye for what he had done, he felt uneasy about just letting his guard down. What if someone else said something tomorrow and they ended up right back where they had started?

He already knew he loved her unconditionally, but he needed time to think, to process, to come to terms with it all.

As though on cue, Theodore came out with the others, heading for their van, all geared up for their raid on Roy. They hailed him as they came and his gaze cut to Sheryl, "I'm sorry. Duty calls."

She shrugged, "It's okay. Plus, I know you need time to decide if I'm worth it. I would feel the same way if you had accused me of such horrible things as I accused you of. Take all the time you need. I just…"

She lifted both shoulders, and then let them drop. He watched her in silence itching to demand, *just what,* but staying silent.

She continued, "I just wanted you to know that I would be here when you get back."

Then before he could guess her intent, she flung herself into his arms and lifted up on tiptoes to plant her lips against his in a kiss. He held himself very still, not daring to respond or even touch her. Her lips moved slowly over his, sending a tingling sensation of awareness all over his body. With a stern inward groan, he tried to will his body not to react, but his traitorous dick jutted out at a ninety-degree angle and pressed against her stomach.

She leaned back, her happy gaze dropping to this unmistakable evidence that he wasn't as indifferent toward her as he was pretending to be.

Wanting to wipe that knowing, feminine grin off her face, he nodded as he wiped his lips with the back of his hand, "I'm counting on you being here when I get back. We should tie up loose ends and I'll escort you to the border myself to be sure you're safe."

The light died in her eyes and she stepped back, her face a mirror of hurt and yet understanding. It was almost as though she was telling him without words that she knew she deserved his treatment of her.

Michael strode toward the van and got in, and the van began to move. Sheryl was still standing where he had left her, staring at the ground and then his heart *did* turn over in his chest. This was Sheryl. No matter how angry she made him, he was unfailingly aware of his love for her. He couldn't bear to leave her in that uncertainty and agony of not knowing more so when he still loved her more than life itself. Besides, he was going off to a mini war with the vampires. He expected to make it back alive and whole but what if anything went wrong?

If it was the last thing he did, he needed to let her know he loved her, he thought.

With a growl, he barked, "Stop the van."

Darryl slid to a smooth stop at once as though he had been expecting the command. The van's door slid open, and Michael jumped out.

"Sheryl," he barked.

She lifted her head, surprise on her features.

He ran to her, seeing the absolute delight spread on her face as he caught her up in his arms and turned her around and around and around and around until she was chortling and giggling like a little girl.

Then he lowered her to her feet and planted a rough, possessive, and yet achingly tender kiss on her lips. She met him hunger for hunger and he realized then that she had been restrained when she had kissed him earlier because she hadn't been sure of her welcome. Her hands traveled in hunger all over his frame just as though they didn't have an audience and his returned the favor. He was hard and ready, and he knew that he wanted to fuck her hard. It would be quick and urgent. It wouldn't be lovemaking; it would be mating.

Shielded by his body from his brothers who were busy catcalling and whistling, Sheryl's hand touched his dick, cupping and squeezing with sexy boldness. The top of his head almost came off with need.

"Oh woman, what you do to me," he groaned against her lips.

She didn't respond. She was too preoccupied with kissing him back.

Finally, they disentangled with evident reluctance. Her eyes were shining as she whispered, "I have a good mind to take you to my room and show you the new lingerie I bought just to say I'm sorry."

He grinned, already interested, "When did you go shopping?"

"While you were still in the meeting and after the girls told me more about what Roy had tried to do to their relationships. I have been such a fool."

He kissed her again, "You're not a fool. You're glorious and wonderful and beautiful and so sexy it blows my mind. You're mine," he finished.

"I'm yours," she agreed.

He tousled her hair, "Send me a picture of that lingerie. I want to be hot and ready for you all the way to battle."

She laughed and kissed his chin, "Give Roy a slap for me."

He chuckled, "I'm a man, baby. We don't do slap fights. I'll punch his lights out."

"My hero," she whispered with a lovelorn expression that made her look so cute and sweet.

Then they had to kiss again to the sound of more screams of encouragement from his brothers.

He left her with a smile, eager to return to her later.

His smile soon vanished as they drew close to the establishment housing close to a hundred vampires faithful to Roy.

The fight was fast, brutal and unfair, as far as Michael was concerned. They had gone in daytime and blasted away the roof of the house. The sun had done the rest, burning the vampires within that house to a crisp in a matter of minutes.

Michael and his brothers surged underground to the inevitable hideouts beneath the main house which were still shielded from sunlight. Their swords slashed this way and that as they fought off throngs of vampires.

Piles of ashes filled the hallway where beheaded vampires immediately turned into ashes and with every slash of his blade, Michael kept looking this way and that for Roy.

A sudden small cry went up from one of the rooms hidden in a small corner of the house and the brothers went to inspect. They found up to fifty vampires, all crouching with their hands up in the classic sign of surrender.

"What is this?" Theodore barked.

The oldest of all the vampires, a woman with long dark hair stood and enunciated in a loud carrying voice, "We are not your enemies."

"Funny you should say that. We've been fending off attacks since we walked in the door," Theodore called.

"We have always lived here in peace. Roy is the one causing trouble. He told so many of the younger vampires that you were the reason they couldn't walk in daylight and they turned on you. I tried to speak to them, but they wouldn't listen. You've wiped out his entire army of vampires. Now, let us go, please," she entreated.

"Aren't these other vampires with you loyal to him?" Connor demanded.

She shook her head mutely.

"How do we know it's true?" Michael asked.

"You don't," she told him. "But please, just trust me."

"Darryl? Anything?" Theodore asked obviously inviting Darryl to use his mindreading skills.

Darryl rolled his eyes, "Like that's gonna work with vampires."

With a sigh, Theodore looked back at the leader of the vampires, "Where's Roy?"

"I heard he went on some sojourn. He believed a former mistress of his father's had another of the Sunlight Rings to give to him," one of the other vampires answered.

"How would you know?" Theodore asked, eyeing the young woman.

She rose to her feet with anger in her eyes, "Because I was his girlfriend until he turned me last night and discarded me. He said I was no good for him anymore. He wants a human girlfriend so he can feed off her when the mood takes him."

The woman sounded bitter, Michael realized. She wouldn't lie about this and certainly not to protect Roy.

"I want all of you gone by nightfall," Theodore decreed.

As they headed back to the van, Michael's phone beeped, and he opened it. He checked his WhatsApp message from Sheryl and his blood went hot. She was reclining against the pillows in a virginal white lingerie made entirely of lace. It contrasted beautifully with the red silk sheets beneath her and the dark brown of her hair.

With a growl, he looked up at his brothers as his arousal and his Wolf stirred, "I'll drive us back to the mansion."

He must have broken all the speed limits because they reached Exotic Rescue with fifteen minutes to spare on the usual travel time from that side of town. As soon as he parked the van, he threw the keys at Darryl and bounded toward the house, eager to see Sheryl. He didn't see his brothers exchange laughing glances behind his back.

As he cleared the foyer, though, his enthusiasm cooled some. Sheryl was standing in the hallway all dressed up, with no lingerie in sight, as she hugged a small girl and a woman who looked eerily familiar.

He cleared his throat a little and Sheryl gave him a dazzling smile when she saw him and ran to hug him. Then she dragged him over to the woman and little girl as she announced, "Come meet my sister Kate and her daughter Marissa."

Sheryl's sister looked a lot like her, he realized, pegging why she looked so familiar. The woman was tall and hand-some, and he guessed she must be the stern sort as she looked him over from head to toe with such an appraising expression that he began to feel like a naughty schoolboy caught with his hand in the cookie jar.

"Well, well," she purred. "This must be the Neanderthal-type guy who doesn't know when to stop staring."

He quirked an eyebrow, "Excuse me?"

She shrugged, "Not my words. It's how Sheryl described you when she wanted to throw me off the scent. But when I couldn't get her on phone for many days, I knew it had to be that you had either kidnapped her and decided never to let her go or you had eloped with her to Vegas anyway for that wedding."

He looked confused as he looked between her and Sheryl.

Sheryl giggled, "Pay her no mind. She loves to throw people off balance."

Kate gave him a warm smile as she came up to him and pulled him into an unexpected hug, "I haven't heard Sheryl laugh like that in years. If you put that joy in her, then I will love you forever."

He stared into the other woman's eyes feeling a kinship and a knowing that they would both do anything to protect Sheryl.

He started to respond when Sheryl gasped and then muttered, "When it rains, it pours."

He looked at her in question and then followed her gaze to the doorway where a tall thin man with a receding hairline was struggling to yank his pants from the grip of a ferocious little kitten. As he watched in disbelief, the man gave the kitten a rough shove that made it and little Marissa cry out.

Marissa ran and picked it up and cradled it in her hands protectively while glaring up at the man with her bottom lip poking out.

The man passed a cold glance over the little girl before plastering a warm smile onto his face and heading straight for Sheryl.

"Darlin', did you miss me?" he called, arms spread wide as though he expected her to fling herself into them.

Sheryl shrank away from him and acting on instincts, Michael planted himself in the man's path, forming a formidable barricade.

Annoyance flashed across the man's features. He couldn't go around Michael because next to Michael's solid frame, he looked like a scrawny party crasher. With the petulance of a child, the newcomer demanded, "Who the hell are you?"

"I think the more important question is, who are you?" Michael countered silkily, arms folded across his chest.

Kate supplied the answer in a tone that dripped ice. "That's *Le Bastard*. Who else would the loser be?"

CHAPTER 16

*S*heryl couldn't quite wrap her mind around what was going on. One minute she had been eagerly looking forward to welcoming Michael with wild midday makeup sex and next thing Kate was calling her and telling her to get her butt downstairs because she was with Marissa in the foyer. She had half-thought it was a prank, but she had come down anyway. She had been shocked and pleased to see her sister and niece.

She hadn't quite finished exclaiming over them when Michael showed up to the party. And now, *Sloan* was here?

How had he known where to find her?

She glared at Kate, "*How* could you do this to me?"

Kate threw up both hands, her face stamped with outraged innocence, "Of course, I didn't. How could you think I would have more than two words to say to this idiot after what he did to you?"

Sheryl wasn't convinced. She narrowed her eyes at her sister.

Sloan eagerly rushed in, "I don't need anyone to find you. I put a tracker on your phone a year ago. All I have to do is open an app," he said, waving his phone around and looking so pleased with himself.

Sheryl sputtered in outrage even as Michael snatched the phone out of Sloan's hand, gave it a cursory glance and carelessly squeezed the phone using his shifter strength until it shattered like glass in his hand.

Sloan howled with outrage. "What did you do that for? You're gonna pay for that."

"No, *you're* gonna pay for what you did to Sheryl," Michael countered.

"Kate take Marissa upstairs to my room," Sheryl directed. She knew that look in Michael's eyes. He badly wanted to deck the guy and right now Sloan *was* asking for it. But she didn't want any violence in front of her little niece.

Kate looked disappointed that she was going to miss the confrontation and she looked like she wanted to reach across and slap the man but of course she couldn't do that with Marissa looking on.

She threw Michael a glance of pure steel that he interpreted as, *Get him for both of us.* Then she turned and guided her daughter upstairs.

Sloan swung first which was exactly what Michael seemed to have been waiting for. His fist was grabbed midair by Michael. Then Michael swung back at him hard, and Sloan grunted with pain as he doubled over.

The next kick was aimed at Sloan's midsection and it carried him straight through the swinging doors and flung him into the courtyard.

Sheryl heard gasps and excited voices, and she rushed out in time to see all the brothers and some workers gathering. She saw her friends as well, Jessica, Julia and Hannah and she sighed as they rushed over to her.

"Is that who I think it is?" Julia breathed.

"Yes ladies. That's *Le Bastard*," she confirmed.

Michael shoved the other man's face into the sand, making him eat dirt in that way children sometimes did, and Sheryl decided she had had enough. It was in no way a fair fight and while Sloan deserved it, she thought it was unnecessary. The point had been made. Sloan was unwelcomed here. Even he couldn't be so obtuse or self-absorbed as not to get the message.

"Michael, stop," she called.

Michael released the other man at once and came to stand beside her.

Gasping, Sloan sat up with his nose and mouth bleeding and his hair and clothes a disheveled mess. Privately Sheryl wondered what she had ever seen in him.

At the same time, she felt a smidgen of pity for him. Whatever else he might have been Sloan had always been very tidy and fastidious about his appearance. She realized then that her feelings for him had been nothing compared to what she felt for Michael. Sloan had evoked nothing more than a passing fondness and attachment, but Michael evoked hot, burning passion and a love so fierce she didn't even know what to do with herself.

He peered up at her, "If you didn't want me here, all you had to do was say so."

She glared, "I'm sure Sally would wonder why you had to ask if I wanted you here or not."

He made a weak motion with one hand. "I'm sorry about Sally. I was an ass. I was wrong. I shouldn't have done that."

Sheryl couldn't believe her ears. Sloan was apologizing?

"I acted without thinking, Sheryl," he said.

"Don't say her name again," Michael warned testily.

And Sheryl realized then that her guy, the love of her life, with his macho build and exceptionally good looks was jealous of the pitiable tiny sap of a man sitting on the ground covered in dust. Men, she thought with a fond smile as she pulled a hand through Michael's elbow and leaned into him.

"You have nothing to worry about my darling. I love you. Always and forever," she whispered for his ears only.

"I wasn't worried," he countered. But she noticed that the scowl on his face did ease somewhat. "And yes Sheryl, I love you too," Michael whispered back.

Her heart warmed by his words, Sheryl faced Sloan. "You know, Sloan, I should be thanking you. If you hadn't done what you did, I wouldn't have met Michael. I wouldn't have known love like this, and I wouldn't be here now. But please go back to your school and to Sally."

Sloan bent his head and began to weep. "I can't go back."

Everyone exchanged confused looks.

"Why can't you go back to the woman you cheated with?" Julia wanted to know. "The woman you couldn't let out of your sight long enough to chase after your hurting fiancée after she caught you in the throes."

Sloan seemed to miss the sarcasm. He raised a tortured ravaged face as he confessed. "Sally didn't want me. She only wanted access to the school's funds. I noticed she and the accountant were skimming a little off the top and when I confronted her about it, she admitted they were in love. I fired her and she reported me for sexual harassment."

"You lost your job?" Sheryl asked.

He nodded.

Theodore's face set in stern lines, "Well, I commiserate with you on the loss of your job, but I'm afraid you cannot stay here. You're not welcome. Guards!"

"Sheryl—" Sloan tried.

"He's right, Sloan," she answered. "Michael and I are together now. There's nothing for you here."

Michael wrapped a possessive arm around her waist, "And what's more, we're getting married. I would invite you to stay for the wedding but Teddy's the boss here. And you heard the man."

The security operatives came forward and lifted the man to his feet. Someone grabbed his little suitcase and in less than a minute he was being marched to the gates and escorted off the property.

Sheryl couldn't get rid of the good feeling in the pits of her stomach. She flicked Michael a surprised glance even as his siblings converged on them to press their felicitations upon them. "We are getting married?" she asked him.

He grinned as he dropped to his knee before her, "That was an unconventional proposal I know. But the thing is Sheryl Quinn, ever since you crashed your way into my life, I've been a goner. I love you and I don't want to be without you. I cannot imagine my life without you even for a nanosecond. So please Sheryl, would you make me the happiest man alive? Would you marry me?"

There was only one answer and her lips formed it happily, "Yes."

Several hours later, Sheryl was still reeling. She still couldn't believe all the events of the day. But she couldn't stem her joy. Who didn't like justice? Sloan had gotten his just desserts and he had gotten to see her happy without him. And best of all, she was deliriously happy and so in love she was almost afraid to believe it.

"I still cannot believe we're getting married," Sheryl announced after they had managed to escape from his congratulating family and hers.

He laughed as he landed on the bed. "Why not? You know all there is to know about me."

He froze as he said the words with the air of someone who just remembered something, and Sheryl's heart sank. "There's something you haven't told me, isn't there?"

He nodded, looking almost ashamed as though it were

something very horrible. Her heart thudded in her chest as she sank onto the bed beside him. "What haven't you told me?"

"I read fast," he confessed in such a low tone that she had to strain to hear him.

Sheryl was confused. "You read fast? How is that a secret? Anyone can read fast."

He looked up at her, "Not like I can. And if we ever have a kid someday, chances are, he or she might inherit that trait and be teased about it in school."

Something didn't add up and she asked, "Like how fast are we talking?"

"I only need twenty minutes to finish a two-hundred-page book," he told her.

If she weren't already sitting down, she would have sat down immediately. Now, she saw why he was reluctant to confess that. Most people would think him a freak. She swallowed carefully, choosing her words with care, because she sensed that whatever she said next would be remembered forever.

"Do your brothers know?"

He shook his head, "Only Theodore."

She caught her hand in his, "I think it's amazingly cool and mind-blowing. That explains why you're so intelligent. I knew you were special, Michael, but each time I learn more about you, I'm blown away by just how special you are. I would be very honored and proud if our kids could pick up that trait from you."

He stared at her as though he couldn't believe his ears and her heart turned over in her chest. For all his strength and machismo, he really could be very vulnerable. She saw now why Connor had been so pissed that she had hurt his brother.

Unable to help herself, she leaned forward, and pressed

her lips against his in a soft, sweet kiss. He reacted almost at once. He pulled her closer to him and began to whisper disjointed avowals of love against her lips as he kissed her with the kind of passion he had never shown her.

Sheryl clutched him to her, exulting in his touch and caresses and passion as he lowered her to the bed.

"You're the most beautiful woman in the world," he declared, his eyes shining down at her.

She chuckled, "You might not think so when you hear my last secret."

He grinned at her, "Try me."

She chuckled, "I have a bald patch somewhere in the middle of my hair. It didn't fall off or something. Hair just never grew there from the day I was born."

He laughed and bent to kiss her nose as he declared arrogantly, "Stale news. I discovered it the first time we made love."

Then he took her lips in another kiss that transported both of them to realms of ecstasy.

"We should make love in a real bed for once," she moaned in approval as he stripped her clothes off her body and hurriedly shed his.

"I want you to make love to me this time honey. Ride me hard," he grunted as he flipped and let her stay on top.

Sheryl giggled as she straddled him, "I like a man who knows how to submit in bed."

Then she guided his hard thrusting dick into her tight wet sheath and all laughter fled. Michael extended one hand and began to flick her clitoris with the pad of his thumb as she began to move up and down on his hard shaft.

His hands alternatively caressed her breasts, cupping them as they bounced every time she moved. Then she slowed and lifted off him.

"Don't stop," he pleaded.

Her grin dripped with pure wickedness. "Something tells me you'll like the reason I stopped. You're gonna like it a lot."

With an eager cry, Sheryl grabbed his thick, fat, dick and put her lips around the head. Michael moaned with pleasure, and she immediately began to pump up and down on his dick, taking as much of him as she could into her mouth. He almost exploded right then judging by the way he jerked in her arms and then grabbed her head with both hands and held on.

Smiling against his penis, Sheryl thrust out her pink, wet velvety tongue and licked his thick dick in a straight line from the base to the very tip. She caressed the ridge formed by the frenulum, flicking her tongue this way and that, this way and that. His grunt of pleasure was so encouraging that she did it again, and again, and again. Her gaze landed on a cup of ice cream sitting on her dresser, and she reached over and shoved a spoonful into her mouth before bending over to take him in her mouth again.

The change in temperature went through Michael in shocking waves and he screamed outright. By this time, he was shaking, his powerful shoulders trembling and rocking with the force of trying to hold onto his fragile control.

She flicked his frenulum and peppered his tip with kisses again. A guttural cry was wrung from his lips, "Please baby."

Sheryl nodded, knowing what he was asking for. She opened her mouth and took him in again more deeply. The tip of his dick was dripping with precum moisture making it so wet, hard, and smooth. Her tongue glided over Michael's dick as she sucked him hard, milking every last drop of moisture. He moaned long and hard at the exquisite pleasure; then his control seemed to break as he grabbed her head and began thrusting hard into her mouth, moaning with every thrust.

While he thrust into her mouth, Sheryl grabbed his balls

and gently began to massage them, prompting him to thrust even faster. After some time, she grabbed hold of his thighs, signaling that she wanted him to stop; then when he slowed, she pulled her mouth away and smiled at his dick which was glistening wetly with saliva and moisture.

"Fuck, baby. Fuck," he growled as he spread her with an urgency on the bed and positioned himself between her legs.

Her pussy was pink and swollen, her clitoris protruding through the folds like a sexy pout. Her musky scent rose to tickle his nose and Michael leaned down to rub his nose against her clit.

He shoved into her on one sure thrust that buried him inside her to the hilt. Then he began to move rapidly making love to her harder and faster and deeper as pleasure carried both of them on its wings and sailed over into another world of deep sighs, moans and satisfaction.

"Are you enjoying it?" he demanded.

"A little too much," she assured him.

He grinned and changed the angle of his thrusts slightly in a way that pressed his hard, long, fat dick against her G-spot.

"Yes, yes, there," she gasped, gripping his forearms with her hands as he made wild passionate love to her.

He bent to nuzzle her cheeks, kissing her and stroking as he continued to fuck her hard.

Her body arched in a tight bow beneath his as she started coming again. His cries of pleasure swallowed hers and soon Michael was also shooting his wet oozing cum into her pussy. His cum was so much that it even began to trickle down her thighs as he finally pulled out of her. Sweat dripped down his back, evident of the energy of his thrusts and he collapsed beside her on the bed, sated, spent, and satisfied.

Sheryl rolled into his arms, burying her face in his neck as the air conditioner cooled their naked bodies.

"That was one hell of a lovemaking," he ventured.

She chuckled, "If the next fifty years are like this, it would be a wonder if either of us ever get out of bed to do anything else."

As they cuddled, she asked, "Why is Connor so protective of you then, if he doesn't know about your fast reading."

Michael sighed, "I lost a partner Eddie. He was one of us in Special Ops. At a point he became withdrawn and depressed. I think he had some issues in his love life. I should have known better that night, but I let him go back into the field. He didn't make it. He got careless and some rogue vampires got the jump on him."

Her throat closed up in sympathy. She could imagine how he must have felt. "I'm so sorry Michael."

He shrugged, "I lost it for a while after that. I went crazy … became over-protective. I think, in some way, that's why I went as far as kidnapping you just to keep you safe. I couldn't stand to see another innocent person injured on my watch because I didn't do enough."

Now, his penchant for excessive control of the odds and over protectiveness made sense. She grabbed him, pulled him down, and kissed him hard.

He lifted his head and looked at her in mute surprise.

"That was for being you Michael. You care about people a lot. It's part of why you were so determined to save me from myself. Thank you for kidnapping me," she added.

It was the most ludicrous statement and he burst into laughter unable to help himself. She joined him, pressing against him as they shared their humor like everything else. His gaze met hers and the molten lava leaped in his golden gaze as they blazed into hers.

She was still laughing when he pressed a gentle kiss to her

lips that made her laughter fade and passion rise inside of her again. To her shock, she felt the steadily hardening pressure of the dick pressed against her side and she widened her eyes in disbelief.

"Well, if this means we're gonna be screwing like rabbits till we die, I suppose that's one hell of a way to go," he said as she rolled her onto his frame and guided his dick into her sopping wet pussy again.

* * *

THE STERN, BEAUTIFUL WOMAN OPENED THE DOOR AN INCH and peeked out with one eye. She glared when she saw who it was. "How dare you show your ugly face here?"

Roy grinned at her, exuding charm and good humor. He knew he had to be graceful and humble. It was the only way in hell he could get her to give him what he wanted: his father's other Sunlight Ring. It was the only prayer he had in hell of getting back to Angel Springs and teaching Theodore Cooper and those Exotic Bastards a lesson.

He had heard the news that Michael and his bitch were getting hitched. Well, he would give them a wedding present of his own, he decided. He had already asked the mole in Exotic Rescue to take pictures of the happy couple for him. He would get it framed and courier it to them. This picture would be worth a million words because one look and they would get the message that Roy Davies hadn't given up. They would know at once that he still had his eyes on them. If that didn't ruin their honeymoon, he didn't know what else would.

But first, I have to get this frog-faced witch to part with the ring my stupid father entrusted to her, he thought, expanding the fake smile on his face as he looked at the woman glaring at him.

"Come now, Rosie," he cajoled in a whiny tone that was rusty from lack of use. "You know you don't really hate me. You're only angry I spurned your advances all those years ago. Well, I've come to give you what you've always wanted," he decreed, stroking a hand with lewd suggestion down his zipper.

The woman flicked him a bored, disinterested look as she ordered, "Strip."

He didn't bother asking if she meant right there on her doorstep; he knew she did. That was Rosie. She always said what she meant. He let his clothes pool at his feet.

Her experienced eyes scanned him, fastening with greed on his hard, jutting dick.

Then with a grin, she opened her door wider and said expansively as though inviting him in for coffee, "Well, don't just stand there. Come on in. *Mi casa, es su casa.*"

EPILOGUE

The wedding was well attended and as Sheryl walked down the aisle to her future husband, she knew she would remember this day for the rest of her life for several reasons.

First, she was getting married to the only man on Earth who knew just how to love her; next, she was keeping some very important news to herself that she couldn't wait to share with Michael. She knew he could be depended upon to be absolutely ecstatic.

He looked dashing and handsome as she walked up to him and she could barely still the wild pounding of her heart as she tried in vain to get him to look anywhere else but at her.

Something about him and his eyes affected her a lot, she thought. He had only to look up when she walked into a room and she was hot and bothered.

She had insisted on pushing their wedding back by two weeks, refusing to get married in a hastily concocted ceremony, and he had lovingly obliged her.

Now, seeing his beaming smile and hot expression as she

walked down the aisle, Sheryl knew she had made the absolute right decision in marrying him. She had heard of bridal nerves, but strange as it seemed, she had none.

She was super confident and very happy as she met him at the altar and began to promise the rest of her life to him. They had chosen a beachside wedding on the grounds of Exotic Rescue and she thought it was the most beautiful wedding she had ever seen.

Her eyes poured out declarations of love to her new husband as they turned to greet their families and friends.

She saw Hannah watching them with a half-smile on her lips and her heart twisted in sympathy for the other woman. Hannah might be loath to admit it, but she knew the other woman still cared deeply about Michael, but it was always one-sided. She would aim her bouquet at Hannah, Sheryl decided, and she would pray it brought her the luck of a man to call her own.

Her gaze landed on her husband as they turned to lead everyone to the reception and the banquet awaiting them in a sea of buffet tables.

"I am the luckiest man alive," he said once he caught her gaze.

Sheryl grinned, "Yes, you are. The luckiest husband *and father.*"

He froze in his tracks and looked at her, his eyes filled with happy questions. Their guests all froze too, sensing something was up as they looked at the couple.

Sheryl nodded, and it was as though that was the signal. Michael hooted with laughter and picked her up and began to swing her in one of those wide, exuberant circles he did so well, laughing and laughing and laughing the whole time like an absolute maniac.

When he lowered her to her feet, he pressed a delicate, barely there kiss onto her lips. It was so achingly tender and so sweet. It was unlike any kiss he had ever given her in the past, and Sheryl grinned as she absorbed the love and warmth radiating off him like the tender rays of the sun directed at a beloved flower.

"I never knew it was possible to be happier than I was a few moments ago when you pledged to love me forever," he whispered. "I love you, baby."

Sheryl grinned up at him, feeling like an absolute fool in love. She just couldn't stop smiling even if she tried.

"I love you too, honey," she told him.

"All right, let's dance," someone called.

All the guests in the room began to move toward the little space left for dancing as though they had been waiting for that very cue all night.

Sheryl let Michael take her in his arms, his eyes shining with gentle pride and possessiveness.

"I thought we came here for the food," she laughed.

"Baby trumps food," he told her.

Sheryl frowned, "We're dancing."

"Yeah. We're celebrating the baby," he informed her.

"And not the wedding?"

He grinned, "Baby, once I get you alone, we're going to celebrate the wedding so hard you might just end up pregnant."

"I'm already pregnant," she frowned.

"So? Haven't you heard of people getting pregnant while already pregnant?"

She shook her head, "You've been watching too much Grey's Anatomy, haven't you?"

"Sheryl, you brought so much light and love into my life. I can't wait to be alone with you."

Sheryl snuck a look around. Most of the guests were dancing, drinking, eating, or all three at the same. No one was paying much attention to them.

"Who says you have to wait to get me alone?" she demanded.

He looked down at the twinkle in her eyes and he chortled, "You're not thinking what I'm thinking, are you?"

Sheryl's eyes twinkled at him as she replied, "A quickie somewhere would make this day memorable."

He flicked Theodore a glance. Theodore was preoccupied with his daughter and Jessica's two kids. Then he smiled down at his bride, "I've always fantasized about messing around in Theodore's office. He's always too serious and treats that goddamn office like some hallowed sanctuary."

"What are we waiting for then?" she laughed with impish delight.

A few minutes later, they had snuck into Theodore's office and slammed the door shut behind them.

Sheryl started to undo her zipper, but Michael caught her hands in his, "Woman, have you ever had an actual quickie?"

He turned her to lean against the wall and he wrestled the material of her dress up to expose bare ass cheeks. He stared in shock for a minute at her ass and then he whistled, "You were naked the whole time at our wedding?"

A saucy grin was the response, "Come get me, Tiger."

That was all the encouragement he needed as he positioned her for his entry and plunged into her wet, willing pussy in one hard thrust as he proceeded to make her his for all time.

The End

* * *

THANK YOU SO MUCH FOR READING CAPTIVE TO HER FATED Mate! We hope you loved it! If you did then we think you will love the Damaged Pack series!

Get the Damaged Pack HERE on Amazon!

It's been years since the Damaged Pack were together...but now with their home town in danger it is time for them return to protect what is theirs...

The adventure begins when Kelly agrees to join her rich best girlfriend on an all expenses African safari She welcomed the chance to forget about her dead end life, and the weight of caring for a young son under the constant pressure of having to make ends meet, all while dealing with a crazy ex to boot! Little did she know what she was getting into...

Derek is not like other men. So much so that the only place he can find peace - the only place his beast can find peace - is on the African savanna, far from the little midwestern town that he has tried so hard to push from memory. The pain and damage of his youth - and his sense of loyalty - are not so easily forgotten though. When another of his old Damaged Pack raises the alarm, he knows he must return to help the one man who gave them all a chance...

Will this unlikely pair be able to navigate their own damage in time to save his home town? Can they save the one man that believed in Derek and shaped his Damaged Pack in his youth? Can they save themselves?

Come and join this adventure with Derek, Kelly and the rest of the Damaged Pack as they each find their mates and then unite to defend everything they hold dear...

Here is a brief preview of the first story in the Damaged Pack series, Return of the Wolf...

"The old man may be in trouble."

Seven simple words and yet their effect was so powerful that the man listening at the other end of the line immediately surged to his feet, his throat dry as he demanded with a croak, "Bo, what the hell does that mean?"

Those words from Bo put Derek in a serious sweat because of the entire Damaged Pack, Bo was the most taciturn and least given to exaggeration.

"Calm down, Derek. I said, he *may* be in trouble. I'm not certain yet."

There was no need to explain who "the old man" was. Derek knew Bo meant Joshua, the craggy old man they had all come to love and respect like a father. Joshua was more than a mentor; he had picked them all up off the streets—all five of them. He'd dusted them off and set them on the right track to being amazing people with something to offer the world. When they had all discovered they had magical abilities that allowed them to turn into different mythical creatures, Joshua had been the one to teach them to hone their strengths; he had taught them to hide their abilities from humans. He had taught them to watch each other's backs, and when the five of them had voted to name themselves the Damaged Pack of Weirna, Joshua had cheered them on.

Derek ground his jaw testily. Why was Bo playing semantics? He had known Bo since he was a kid, and not once had he caught the other man in a lie or an exaggeration. If Bo said the old man may be in trouble, it meant the old man was in the very thick of it! Bo was the master of understatements.

For all his wonderful traits, Joshua Cox was also a very stubborn old man. He would never admit that he needed help. And Bo was just as stubborn, Derek thought in exasperation. If Bo was calling now, then he obviously needed help with Joshua's problem, but he would die before he would admit it.

There was only one possible solution.

"I'll be on the next plane out!" Derek ground out. The words were tight in his throat as memories of Weirna threatened. It was the only real home he had ever known, but then it had turned out to be his doom too. He shoved the memories aside; he needed to focus more on the good and on Joshua.

"Hey, hold your horses," Bo interjected in a gruff tone. "You don't need to do that— yet."

"Why not?"

"Things haven't progressed to that point just yet. Heck, I haven't even contacted any of the others as it is."

"What's been going on, Bo?" Derek demanded.

"I'm not sure. Just some vibes I picked up. I'm gonna watch him a little more and get back to you."

"I'll call you in two days."

"Two weeks, Derek. Give me two weeks. Oh, and you won't be able to reach me. I'll reach you."

The line went dead.

"Yo man, they're here," someone shouted as Derek returned his phone to his pocket, deep in thought.

He raised his head slightly, sniffed the air a little and then relaxed. The little crowd of ten people were next to harmless; one sniff could tell him loads about an entire room full of people. It was his unique gift.

Derek looked around at his surroundings; natural vegetation on every side, just the way he liked it. Tall forest trees, dense shrubs, the scent of rotting leaves, faint scent of dried animal blood, and wet earth; he was in his element.

He looked at the men, women and two kids assembled before him; they were tourists looking for a good time in the wilds of Kenya. Dexen Resort was his idea; his and his partners'. They had set it up in a place few tourist resorts dared to use. The area was closer to the jungles of Kenya and offered exposure to more wildlife and the government had been on the verge of cordoning it off when he had appeared and offered to buy it. They had been dumbfounded but when he had managed to drum up financial support from his partners, they had gladly let him have it. The area was wild and untamed but with funding and help from his partners, he had made the resort into a luxurious paradise. It had become a veritable Mecca for the more adventurous tourists because Derek was famed for taking tourists to places where angels feared to tread and bringing them back safe and sound. No wild animal had ever harmed anyone he was leading around. In a matter of three years, Derek and Dexen Resort had quickly become sought-after throughout Kenya. He had been travelling all over Africa for the past decade, picking up experiences and adventure; the last three years, he had settled in Kenya.

He loved Kenya. It offered one of the most exotic wildlife tourisms of any place on earth and something about the African country and its virgin, raw, naked appeal drew him and enthralled every last one of his senses.

Ever since he had come here as a wildlife tour guide, he hadn't looked back. He had adapted so fast and become so knowledgeable about the area, and even the language, that all the locals loved him. Everywhere he went, local women pressed food on him, and young local girls tried to rub their breasts against his arm, their dark eyes filled with silent, wicked promises smiling into his.

He made it a point to avoid them all. He alone knew his powerful secret; he alone knew he could lose all control in the throes of passion. It had happened once with Marjorie; she had discovered his secret and ultimately he had lost her forever.

He smiled a warm welcome now at the assembled tourists in front of him, unleashing his fatal attraction on the gathered crowd with his potent dimpled smile that eased his chiseled features.

Derek was very tall, at six-three, with a mass of long black hair that hung to his shoulders and was tied up at his nape with a band. His eyes were an unsettling shade of grey that tended to turn pure silver when he was in a mood — and he *was* in a mood more than half the time. Marjorie had described him in that lilting Spanish-accented voice of hers as the "tall, dark, brooding sort with animal magnetism."

The thought of Marjorie made his heart squeeze in his chest and he shut his eyes for a minute, allowing himself to picture her with her short, wispy blond hair, exotic green eyes, and throaty laugh. He wanted desperately to have her in his arms again, just like in the old days; to sniff her unique shampoo and kiss her chubby cheeks until she chortled. With a tired sigh, he forced his eyes open— hell had a better chance of freezing over before any of that would happen. Besides, at this point, he wasn't necessarily fantasizing about Marjorie; just any beautiful woman! He had been celibate for more than a decade, thanks to Marjorie!

"Welcome!" he got out, focusing his attention on the men and women assembled in front of him.

Choruses of "Hi," and "Hello" rent the air.

"You guys ready for our tour? It's gonna be amazing," Derek said, smiling at the small group. They were two American couples, an African couple and a Chinese couple and they all seemed very eager to get started. Two little kids, a boy and a girl, were also hanging onto their mothers' hands, dressed from head to toe in protective clothing.

He hid a grin. He had taken special care of the area and it was as safe as could be. But then, they were tourists; he supposed the slight niggling fear at the back of their minds was part of the excitement. Adventure was supposed to come with some small dread in the pit of your stomach, wasn't it? Fear was good in this context; otherwise, their outing would just be a snooze-fest.

Something shifted in the wind; he tensed, inhaling deeply as a wild, indefinable scent quivered on the edge of his senses. It was sweet and tangy and strangely intense, and it seemed to go straight to his brain! What *was* that? Before he could fathom what it was, a fresh gust of wind blew right into his face and he lost the scent.

"I'm Derek Cavanaugh," he told the tourists, forcing his attention back to them. "I'll be your tour guide today. The area is pretty much safe but because I'll be showing you a lot of hidden caves and paths and wild animals, I don't want anyone to get lost or hurt, so you have to do exactly what I say every time, okay?" he finished as he turned to lead the way.

"Hey, hold up," someone called, laughing breathlessly as a group of three people ran up to them. "Tom lost his shoe, so we got held up."

Derek turned, along with everyone else. Two women and a little boy were approaching the group. The woman who had spoken was clad in tee-shirt and jeans with a pair of glasses shading her eyes. Despite her casual appearance, he could tell she was extremely wealthy. She had that aura of quiet wealth about her, and she walked with the confident gait of the average wealthy American.

Beside her, another woman tagged along with her son in tow. The second woman was wearing an unbuttoned shirt over a tank top and jeans with scuffed sneakers. She had a fresh, unspoiled face, and even from a distance, and devoid of makeup, he could tell she was a total knockout. As she walked forward, her chin-length red hair fluttered in the slight wind again and her scent blew his way, hitting him in the solar plexus like a blow.

Derek tensed, every fiber of his being going on high alert as he inhaled the second woman's scent. That was the exact scent he had picked up earlier; it was unlike anything he had ever perceived in his entire life. It was calming and drugging at the same time; it made him want to bury his nose in her skin and hair for the rest of his life; it stoked a hunger deep in his soul, and at the same time, satisfied him. Everything inside of him roared with need. That wild, dangerous side of him reared its head; snapping to be free. His eyes glinted in warning, his teeth started to shift, and with great effort, he clenched his fists to control himself.

Through narrowed eyes, he observed that she was a deliciously stacked woman, with curves in all the right places. She was about five-eight, with slim, delicate shoulders that made a man want to protect her, smooth flawless skin like a baby, high arched brows, high cheekbones that defined her slim face and aquamarine eyes that were so startling in their intensity that even from several feet away he was struck. And yet, there was a sad quality in her eyes; barely there but he saw it. Her breasts were high and firm beneath her tank top and her tiny waist gave room to curvy hips encased in jeans so tight she seemed to have been poured into them. She was incredibly hot and ... *rather dangerous*, he thought— she had to be, because why else would she affect him like this?

Everything in him was raring, straining to be free.

The women came closer, heedless of his inner turmoil, and Derek realized, for the first time in his life, that if he didn't beat a hasty retreat, he could shift form right there in front of everyone.

Derek took a few hasty steps back for self-preservation; the little group kept coming closer. He saw Murphy, his co-guide, shoot him a confused look.

"I'm gonna be sick," he got out desperately. Before anyone could so much as comment, he lunged for the back of the resort and disappeared from view.

He ran off into the dense forest behind the resort and grabbed the first strong oak he came to. He shook it hard, shaking it until it began to uproot from the ground. His entire skin was on fire as the familiar heat spread through him.

What was it about that woman that had made him lose all control? At thirty, he had mastered himself enough that he never once shifted form, unless he absolutely wanted to or unless it was a full moon. Today, though, one whiff of a woman's scent and he had lost all control and had been about to reveal his secret.

Okay, not just any woman; this woman!

What was wrong with him? Who was she?

He gave the tree one last vigorous shake as he felt his wild side begin to recede some more. *I am under control now,* he thought as he slowly let go of the tree.

He'd wanted to have her in his arms with a desperation that defied all logic. He'd wanted to revel in her unique scent and bite her cheeks and lick every part of her in the most sensuous way possible — and he didn't even know her name! What the hell was wrong with him?

CONTINUE THIS ADVENTURE AND READ THE DAMAGED PACK SHIFTERS HERE on Amazon...

www.ingramcontent.com/pod-product-compliance
Lightning Source LLC
Chambersburg PA
CBHW072224150726
48002CB00005B/1944